A writer of "incredible b[...] York Times bestselling author LaVyrle Spencer offers a story to cherish—about falling in love and finding the courage to follow your dreams . . .

Lee Walker knows it won't be easy to start a new life in a new city. But she is on a mission: to prove to everyone, and to herself, that she can make it here, working in the masculine world of the construction industry . . .

When contracting rival Sam Brown offers her a job, Lee is stunned . . . and a little wary. Sam's motives seem honorable enough, even if he doesn't see her in a strictly professional light. In fact, Sam sees her as the woman she's always hoped to be—smart, capable, warm, and funny. And sexy. Before she knows it, Lee is falling head over heels for her boss . . . but part of her is sure that telling Sam about her past would have him backing away, fast. Now she must choose between protecting her bruised and battered heart—or trusting it to a man whose quiet strength just might heal it . . .

"[LaVyrle Spencer] knows how to tug at readers' heart-strings."   —*Publishers Weekly*

Affaire de Coeur

continued . . .

The Endearment

A woman's love is threatened by past secrets . . . "A tender, sensual story."   —Lisa Gregory

Morning Glory

Two misfit hearts find tenderness . . . "A superb book."
—New York Daily News

Spring Fancy

A bride-to-be falls in love—with another man . . . "Incredible beauty."   *—Affaire de Coeur*

The Hellion

Sparks fly between a lady and a hell-raiser . . . "Superb."
—Chicago Sun-Times

Vows

Two willful lovers—one special promise . . . "Magic."
—Affaire de Coeur

The Gamble

Take a chance on love . . . "Grand."   *—Good Housekeeping*

Years

Across the Western plains, only the strongest survived . . . "Splendid."   *—Publishers Weekly*

Separate Beds

First came the baby, then marriage . . . then love . . . "A superb story."   *—Los Angeles Times*

Twice Loved

A woman's missing husband returns—after she's remarried . . . "Emotional."   *—Rocky Mountain News*

Hummingbird

The novel that launched LaVyrle Spencer's stunning career . . . "Will leave you breathless."   *—Affaire de Coeur*

A Promise to Cherish

LaVYRLE SPENCER

JOVE BOOKS, NEW YORK

THE BERKLEY PUBLISHING GROUP
Published by the Penguin Group
Penguin Group (USA) Inc.
375 Hudson Street, New York, New York 10014, USA
Penguin Group (Canada), 10 Alcorn Avenue, Toronto, Ontario M4V 3B2, Canada
(a division of Pearson Penguin Canada Inc.)
Penguin Books Ltd., 80 Strand, London WC2R 0RL, England
Penguin Group Ireland, 25 St. Stephen's Green, Dublin 2, Ireland (a division of Penguin Books Ltd.)
Penguin Group (Australia), 250 Camberwell Road, Camberwell, Victoria 3124, Australia
(a division of Pearson Australia Group Pty. Ltd.)
Penguin Books India Pvt. Ltd., 11 Community Centre, Panchsheel Park, New Delhi—110 017, India
Penguin Group (NZ), Cnr. Airborne and Rosedale Roads, Albany, Auckland 1310, New Zealand
(a division of Pearson New Zealand Ltd.)
Penguin Books (South Africa) (Pty.) Ltd., 24 Sturdee Avenue, Rosebank, Johannesburg 2196, South
Africa

Penguin Books Ltd., Registered Offices: 80 Strand, London WC2R 0RL, England

A PROMISE TO CHERISH

A Jove Book / published by arrangement with the author.

PRINTING HISTORY
First Jove mass-market edition / February 1983
Second Jove mass-market edition / December 2004

Copyright © 1983 by LaVyrle Spencer.
Cover design by Rich Hasselberger.
Cover illustration by Jim Griffin.
Interior text design by Kristin del Rosario.

For information address: The Berkley Publishing Group,
a division of Penguin Group (USA) Inc.,
375 Hudson Street, New York, New York 10014.

ISBN: 0-515-13857-6

JOVE®
Jove Books are published by The Berkley Publishing Group,
a division of Penguin Group (USA) Inc.
375 Hudson Street, New York, New York 10014.
JOVE is a registered trademark of Penguin Group (USA) Inc.
The "J" design is a trademark belonging to Penguin Group (USA) Inc.

PRINTED IN THE UNITED STATES OF AMERICA

10 9 8 7 6 5 4 3 2 1

*With
gratitude
to my friends in
Independence and Kansas City—
Bea, who gave me the map
Barbra, who showed me the old orchard
and
Vivien Lee, who took me to the "C C"*

A Promise to Cherish

Chapter
ONE

As the first suitcase came clunking down the luggage return of Stapleton International Airport in Denver, Lee Walker checked her watch impatiently, drummed four coral fingernails against her shoulder bag, and studied the conveyor belt with a frown. It moved like a sedated snail! She glanced at her watch a second time—only one hour and ten minutes before the bid letting! If the damn suitcase didn't roll out soon, she'd end up at City Hall in these faded blue jeans!

Lee glowered at the flapping porthole until at last her suitcase came through. She sighed deeply and strained to reach it.

She plucked it off the conveyor belt and flew—a

tall, dark-skinned flash of loose black hair and aqua feathers, the worn patches on the backside of her tight jeans attracting the eyes of several men she adroitly sidestepped. The feathers in her hair lifted with each long-legged slap of her moccasins on the terminal floor until she came at last, panting and winded by the thin Denver air, to the Economy Rent-A-Car booth.

Twenty minutes later the same suitcase hit the bed in Room 110 of the Cherry Creek Motel. Lee reached to yank the shirttails free of her jeans at the same time that she released the catch on the suitcase and flipped it open. Her hand halted. Her jaw dropped open.

"Oh my God," she whispered. Lifeless fingers forgot about buttons. Stricken eyes stared at the strange contents of the suitcase while one hand covered her lips, the other clasped her suddenly queasy stomach. "Oh sh . . ." Her eyes took it in, but her mind balked. "No . . . it can't be!" But she was staring not at the mustard-colored envelope containing the bid for a sewage treatment plant she'd worked on for the last two weeks. Instead, a half-naked blonde tootsie lifted a pair of enormous breasts and smiled a come-hither message from the cover of a . . . a *Thrust* magazine.

For a moment Lee was struck motionless with disbelief. *Thrust?* She stood hunched over, horrified, her thoughts whirling. Then frantically she scrambled through the suitcase, throwing out item after item—a gray sweat suit, two pair of dress trousers, a man's shaving kit, two neatly folded shirts, royal blue jockey shorts—*royal blue?*—black socks, Rawhide deodorant, a pair of well-worn jogging shoes with filthy laces, a hair blower, and a brush with very dark brown hair caught in its white bristles.

She ran a thumb over them, then dropped it distastefully and quit scrambling through the contents to grab the identification tag dangling from the suitcase handle.

Sam Brown
8990 Ward Parkway
Kansas City, Missouri 64110

With a groan Lee sank to the bed, leaned forward, and clutched her forehead in both hands. *Oh, damn my hide, I've really done it now. Old Thorpe will gloat over this for months!* At the thought of Thorpe and his small, racist mind, panic swept Lee, tightening the skin across her temples, making the blood sing and swirl crazily as she burst to her feet. She checked her watch. Frantic thoughts tumbled about in her head, leaving her to stand in indecision, glancing from phone to suitcase to the car keys on the bed.

Countless dire possibilities insinuated themselves into Lee's thoughts while she wondered who to call first. Could she possibly retrieve her own suitcase and make it to the bid letting before two o'clock?

She wasted five minutes telephoning the airline's passenger information, who told her to call lost and found, who informed her they'd get back to her in half an hour. Frustrated and angry at both herself and the airline, which hadn't had an attendant checking baggage-claim stubs, Lee finally returned to the airport. When a search of the baggage department proved futile, there seemed little to do except call the home office in Kansas City and admit her blunder.

Lee's stomach churned as she dialed. She pictured the fat belly and seedy little eyes of Floyd Thorpe, the company president and owner, who never lost an opportunity to remind Lee exactly why he'd hired her. Oh, he'd been waiting for this. Like the self-righteous bigot he was, how he'd been waiting. She knew full well Thorpe gritted his teeth every time they passed each other in the office. He probably visited his psychotherapist every payday after signing her check.

Well, you wanted to compete in a man's world and earn a man's salary, and you are!

But never in her three years in the construction industry had Lee earned it so dearly.

Floyd Thorpe's voice fairly shook with rage. He let out a blue streak of cuss words, ending with an order for Lee to "get your liberated female ass to that bid letting and find out who the hell was low bidder, and when you have, get on the next plane home because I'm not—by God—paying for any goddam *woman* to stay in a Colorado motel and eat on my company expense account when she doesn't know her ass from a catch basin, and any government bureaucrat who think it's easy to find *minority* employees who are worth diddly can shove his Minority Business Enterprise Goals—"

That's where Lee hung up.

Sexist, bigoted bastard! she raged silently, feeling again the ineffable futility of trying to change the jaundiced views of men like Floyd A. Thorpe.

Lee had no delusions about why she'd been hired. Not only was she a woman, she was also one-quarter American Indian, and either fact qualified her employer as a minority contractor in the eyes of the federal government as long as she was a corporation officer or owner. Furthermore, the federal government had proclaimed that ten percent of all federal monies allocated for public improvements were to be paid to minority contractors.

Considering the marked advantage of those contractors in today's business world, Floyd A. Thorpe would have given the diamonds out of the opera windows of his Diamond Jubilee Lincoln Continental Mark V to be an Indian woman himself—if he could possibly manage it without being red and female! But

Floyd Thorpe was not only male, he was also as Cau-
casian as the president himself, and he never let Lee
forget it. Whenever she was around, he spit juice
from the ever-present poke of tobacco that bulged his
cheek. He hoisted up his pot belly with strutting tugs
on his overstrained belt. He told dirty jokes and
talked like the sewer rat he was. It got worse and
worse as Lee continued to refuse his invitations to
become a vice-president of Thorpe Construction.
And if Lee Walker didn't like it, Thorpe's overbearing attitude clearly stated, she could go home and
chew hides, plant maize, and raise a few papooses.

As Lee now spun from the telephone and crossed
the airport terminal, she too gritted her teeth. Yes, she
wanted equal pay, so once again she had to lick his
boots and go out there and earn it!

SHE arrived at the bid letting five minutes late. As
usual, she was the only woman in the room. Up
front the city engineer was opening a sealed envelope
as Lee slipped into a folding chair at the back of the
room. From her purse she took a tablet and pen, then
glanced surreptitiously at the lap of the man next to
her as he entered the amount of the bid being read.

She wrote it quickly on her own paper, then leaned
over to ask, "How many have been opened?"

He counted with the tip of a mechanical pencil. "Only six so far."

"Do you mind if I copy them?"

"Not at all."

He angled the pad her way, and Lee took down the six names and amounts. Glancing around the room, she found an unusually large number of contractors represented. The nation's slumping economy, coupled with relatively little new-home construction, had contractors traveling farther and bidding tougher in order to get work.

The Denver suburb of Aurora had attracted much attention, for it was one of the fastest growing mid-size cities in the nation. Aurora had solved its most serious problem—a shortage of water—by obtaining its own water supply and bringing it down from Leadville, a hundred miles away. But that water needed filtering and chemical treatment before use, adequate sewage treatment and removal after use. Every contractor in the room understood the value of getting in on the ground floor of the city's growth. To win this bid would be like plucking the first ripe plum in a highly productive orchard.

Suddenly Lee's back stiffened as the voice of the city engineer rang across the room, reading the name on the front of the next envelope.

"Thorpe Construction Company of Kansas City."

Lee stiffened and her heart did a double-whammy. There must be some mistake! She searched the room for anyone else from Thorpe, but she was the only one present. How could the envelope have gotten there? She scarcely had time to wonder before a brass letter opener sliced through the thick envelope with a raspy sound of authority, and while Lee still floundered in stunned surprise, her bid was read aloud:

"Four million two hundred forty-nine thousand."

Her heart thudded like a bass drum and she pressed a palm against it. *My God! I'm the low bidder so far!* Across the room faces fell as those who'd been beaten out sighed with disappointment.

Lee knew nothing to equal the exhilaration of moments like this. The sweet taste of revenge was already making her mouth water as she thought of returning to Kansas City and flinging the news in the beady little mustard seed eyes of one Floyd A. Thorpe, alias F.A.T., as Lee often thought of him.

Another bid was read: four million six. Hers was still low!

It took every effort to sit calmly in her chair and wait. How often she'd sat in sessions like this and known this giddy elation until someone else bested her at the last moment. There could be only one winner, and the larger the number of submissions, the greater the glory; the larger the job, the greater the possible profits. And this one was big . . .

Lee chewed her lower lip, trying to contain her growing excitement as three more bids were opened and read, none of them lower than hers.

Finally the city engineer grinned and announced the last bid. "Brown and Brown, Inc., Kansas City, Missouri," he said as he lifted the bulky envelope and slit it. The room was as silent as outer space. Even before he read the amount aloud, the city engineer's smile broadened, and Lee experienced a premonition of doom.

"Four million two hundred forty-five thousand!"

The blood seemed to drop to Lee's feet. She wilted against the back of her chair and strove not to let her disappointment show. She swallowed, closed her eyes momentarily, and breathed deeply while the scuffle of shoes and the metallic clank of chairs filled the room. Her body felt like lead, but she forced herself to her feet. To lose was tough. To be second was harder. But to be second by only four thousand dollars on a job worth over four million was agony.

Four thousand dollars—Lee restrained an ironic grunt. It might as well have been four cents!

Could there by anything harder than congratulating the winner at a time like this? The man beside Lee moved toward the cluster of people who'd converged, Lee presumed, around the winning estimator. She caught a glimpse of a dark head, wide shoulders . . . and immediately squared her own.

Protocol, she thought dismally, wishing she could forgo congratulations.

The man was accepting them with obvious relish. His wide smile was turned upon a competitor who railed good-naturedly, "You did it again, Sam, damn ya! Why don't you leave some for the rest of us?"

The smile became a laugh as his darkly tanned hand pumped the much lighter colored one. "Next time, Marv, okay? My luck can't hold forever." Others shook his hand, and exchanged brief business comments while Lee waited her chance to approach him. His wide hand was enclosed around another when his eyes swung to find her in front of him. Those eyes were deep brown in a tan face. Pale crinkles at the corners of his eyes suggested he had squinted many hours into the sun. His nose was narrow, Nordic; the lips widely smiling, pleased at the moment. His neck was thick and his posture more erect than any other man's in the room. Lee had a brief glimpse of a silver and turquoise cross resting in the cleft of his open collar as his shoulders swung her way. His palm slid free of the man still addressing him, as if the brown-eyed winner had forgotten him in the middle of a sentence.

"Congratulations . . . Sam, is it?" Lee extended her hand. His grip was like that of a front-end loader.

"That's right. Sam Brown. And thank you. This one was too close for comfort."

Lee's lips parted and her eyes widened. *Sam Brown?* The coincidence was too great to be believed! *Sam Brown?* The same Sam Brown who read girlie magazines? He certainly didn't look like the type who'd need to.

Lee quelled the inane urge to ask him if he used Rawhide deodorant and instead lifted her eyes to his hair for verification—it was indeed dark brown, straight, and appeared to be blow-combed into the stylish, unparted sweep that touched both ear and forehead and the very tip of his collar. In a crazy-clear recollection, royal blue jockey shorts flashed across Lee's mind, and she felt a flush begin to creep up from her navel.

"You don't have to tell me it was too close for comfort," Lee replied. "I'm the one who just came in second." Sam Brown's palm was hard and warm and captured hers too long. "I'm Lee Walker, Thorpe Construction."

His black brows lifted in surprise, and she freed her hand at last.

"Lee Walker?"

"Yes."

"Of Kansas City?"

"Yes."

The beginning of a grin appeared on his wide lips, and his dark eyes drifted down over her wrinkled plaid shirt, faded jeans, and scuffed moccasins.

On their way back up, they took on a distinct glint of humor.

"I think I have something of yours," he said, leaning a little closer, his voice low and confidential.

Across her mind's eye paraded a file of personal items from her suitcase—bras, pants, tampons, her daily journal. His insinuating perusal made her uncomfortably aware that she was dressed like a teenage runaway while attending a business function requiring professionalism in both comportment and dress. At the same time he—though missing his suitcase, too—was dressed in shiny brown loafers, neat cocoa brown trousers, an open throated peach-colored shirt, and a summer-weight oatmeal-colored sport coat.

The difference made Lee feel at a distinct disadvantage. She felt the heat reach her face and with it a wave of suspicion and anger. Yes he certainly *did* have something of hers—a job worth over four million dollars! But this was no place to accuse him. Other people stood within earshot, thus she was forced to reply with only half the rancor she felt.

"Then it *was* you who turned in my bid."

"It was."

"And I suppose you think I should thank you for it?"

His smile only deepened the indentations on either

side of his lips. "Didn't anyone ever tell you always to carry anything of immediate importance on the plane with you?"

Stung by the fact that he was undeniably right, she could only glare and splutter, "Perhaps you should consider teaching a workshop on the *dos* and *don'ts* of preparing bids for a public bid letting. I'm sure the class could learn innumerable new techniques from you."

He had the grace to back off and decrease the wattage of his grin.

"How dare you turn in someone else's bid!" she challenged.

"Under the circumstances, I felt it the only honorable thing to do."

"Honorable!" she nearly yelped, then forcibly lowered her voice. "You honorably looked it over first, though, didn't you!"

His half grin changed to a scowl. "*You're* the one who got the wrong suitcase. I picked—"

"I don't care to discuss it here, if you don't mind," she hissed in a stage whisper, glancing in a semicircle to find too many curious ears nearby. "But I *do* want to discuss it!" Her eyes blazed, but she forced restraint into her tones, though she wanted to let him have it with both barrels. "Where is it?"

Contrarily he slipped a lazy hand into his trouser

pocket and slung his weight on one hip. "Where is what?"

"My suitcase," she ground out with deliberate diction as if explaining to a dimwit.

"Oh, that." He looked away disinterestedly. "It's in my car."

She waited with long-suffering patience but he refrained from offering to get it for her.

"Shall we trade?" she suggested with saccharine sweetness.

"Trade?" Again his dark gaze turned to her.

"I believe I have something of yours, too."

Now she had his full attention. He leaned closer. "You have *my* suitcase?"

"Not exactly, but I know where it is."

"Where?"

"I returned it to the airport."

His brows curled, and he checked his watch hurriedly. But at that moment an enormous red-faced man clapped a big paw on Sam Brown's shoulder and turned him around. "Sam, if we're going to talk about that subcontract, we'd better get going. I have"—he, too, bared a wrist to check the time—"at the outside, an hour and a half."

Brown nodded. "I'll be right with you, John. Give me a minute." He turned hastily back to Lee. "I'm sorry I have to run. Where are you staying? I'll bring your suitcase no later than six o'clock." He was already easing toward the door.

"Hey, wait a minute, I—"

"Sorry, but I have a previous commitment. What motel?" John was in the doorway, waiting impatiently.

"I have to catch a plane! Don't you dare leave!"

Sam Brown had reached the door. "What motel?" he insisted.

"Damn!" she muttered as her hands gripped her hips, and she all but stamped a foot in frustration. "Cherry Creek Motel, but I can't wait—"

"Cherry Creek Motel," he repeated, and raised an index finger. "I'll deliver it." Then he was gone.

For the next three hours Lee sat like a caged rabbit in Room 110 of the Cherry Creek Motel while her irritation grew with each passing minute. By six o'clock she felt like a time bomb. She was hot and dirty. Denver in July was like an inferno, and Lee wanted nothing so much as a cool, refreshing bath. But she couldn't take one without her suitcase. Old Thorpe was going to be hotter than a cannibal's stewpot when he found out she hadn't returned to Kansas City as ordered. A check on late-leaving flights confirmed that Lee had already missed the suppertime flight, and the next one didn't leave till 10:10 P.M. She was damned if she'd stay up half the night just to get into the office bright and early for Thorpe's self-righteous tirade. After all, it wasn't her fault. And she'd had a harrowing day and still had a bone to pick with the "honorable" Sam Brown.

Every time she thought of him, her temperature rose a notch. To leave her high and dry and sashay off without returning her property was bad enough, but worse was the dirty, underhanded trick he'd pulled with her bid. She couldn't wait to tear into him and tell him exactly what a sneaky, low, lying dog he was!

At 6:15 she stormed to the TV and slammed a palm against the off button. She didn't give two hoots what tomorrow's weather would be like in Denver. All she wanted was to get out of this miserable city!

When a knock finally sounded, Lee's head snapped up and she stopped pacing momentarily, then stormed across and flung the door open.

Sam Brown stood on the sidewalk with two identical suitcases in his hands.

"You're late!" she snapped, glaring up at him with black, angry eyes.

"Sorry I had to run off like that. I got here as soon as I could."

"Well, it's not soon enough. I've already missed my flight, and my boss is going to be livid!"

"I said I was sorry, but you're the one who caused all this by grabbing the wrong luggage at the airport."

"Me! How about you! How dare you run off with my suitcase!"

"As I said before, you ran off with mine."

She gritted her teeth, knowing a frustration so overwhelming it turned her vision blazing red. "I'm not talking about at the airport. I'm talking about after the bid letting. You left me here to sit and stew and not even a brush to brush my hair with or clean clothes so I could take a bath or . . . or . . ." Disgusted, she yanked a suitcase from his hand and flung it onto the bed. Again she spun on him and ordered, "You've got some explaining to do. I'd suggest you begin."

He stepped inside obligingly, closed the door, set the other suitcase down, glanced around, and asked, "May I?" Then, as unruffled as you please, he carefully tugged at the crease in his impeccable pants before easing down in one of the two chairs beside the small round table.

With her hands on her hips, Lee spat out, "No . . . you . . . may . . . not!"

But instead of getting up, he spread his knees, leaned both elbows on them, and let his hands dangle limply between them. "Listen, Miss Walker, it's been a helluva—"

"*Ms*. Walker," she interrupted.

He raised one brow, paused a moment, then repeated patiently, "*Ms*. Walker." He flexed his shoulder muscles, kneaded the back of his neck, and continued, "It's been a long day and I'd like to get out of these clothes."

"You opened my suitcase," she stated unsympathetically, scarcely able to keep her temper under control.

"I what?"

She leaned forward and riveted him with snapping, black eyes. "You opened my suitcase!"

"Why, hell yes, I opened it. I thought it was mine."

"But you did more than just open it! You looked through it!"

"Oh did I, now?"

"Are you denying it?"

"Well, what about you? Are you saying you didn't open mine?"

"Don't change the subject!"

"The subject, I believe, is suitcases, and women who are sore losers."

"Sore losers . . . *sore losers!*" She stepped closer, towering over him. "Why, you lying, cheating . . . crook!" she shouted.

"What the hell are you driving at, *Ms.* Walker?"

"You opened my suitcase, found my unsealed bid, saw that it already had all the necessary signatures, looked it over, and undercut me by a stinking four thousand dollars, then played the benevolent Good

Samaritan by turning in my envelope at the bid letting . . ."

In one swift motion Sam Brown came up out of his chair, swung her around, and stabbed two blunt fingers in the middle of her chest. The poke sent her reeling backward till she landed with an undignified bounce on the bed.

"That's a mighty serious allegation, lady!"

"That's a mighty narrow margin . . . *man!*" she sneered, leaning back on her hands as he stood above her, one of his knees pressing hard against hers. His face wore a thunderous look, made all the more formidable by the swarthiness of his skin and brows. Suddenly, though, he backed off, hands on hips as he cast a deprecating glance along her length.

"Oh, one of those," he intoned knowingly.

She rebounded off the bed, planted a palm on his chest, shoved him back two feet, stepped around him, then faced him squarely.

"Yes, one of those. I'm sick and tired of men who think a woman can't compete in this all-male sewer and water industry of theirs!"

"That's not what I meant when I called you lady, so don't put ulterior meanings on it."

"Oh, isn't it? Then why did you make the distinction? Isn't it because once you realized that suitcase belonged to a woman, you also realized the bid must have been prepared by a woman and you couldn't face getting stung at a public bid letting by losing to her?"

He pointed a long brown finger at her nose and leaned at a dangerous angle from the hip.

"Lady . . ." he began, but cut the word in half and tried again. "Ms. Walker, you're an opinionated, egotistical . . . suffragette! What makes you think nobody else in the world can bid a job better than you?" He began pacing in the small space before the table and chairs. "My God, take a look at the economy, at the number of contractors who are folding every month. Count the number who showed up at that bid letting today. That job will keep crews working for an entire season! Everybody wanted it. The margin was bound to be narrow!"

"Four thousand on four million is too narrow to be accidental, especially from a man who had possession of my suitcase during the earlier part of the day."

A look of pure disgust turned his features to granite. He stood before her, stalk still, jaw clamped tight. Momentarily his expression altered to a heavy-lidded perusal. His lips softened. His eyes traveled slowly down the madras shirt, not quite reaching her hips before starting back up again. His voice fell to a distasteful purr as he backed a step away and mused with strained male tolerance. "From what I saw in your suitcase, it's to be expected you'd be testy at this time of the month, so I'll chalk this up to female taboos and won't take further issue over your ch—"

Crack!!

She smacked him across the side of the mouth with an open palm. It knocked him momentarily off balance, and he teetered back in stunned surprise.

"Why . . . you . . . degenerate," she grated. "I might have expected something like that out of a . . . pervert who carried porno magazines in his suitcase on a business trip!"

Four red stripes in the shape of her fingers appeared to the left of his lips. His fists clenched. The cords along his neck stood at attention. His eyes glowered like chips of resin, and his lips were a thin, tight line.

Fear coursed through Lee at her own temerity. What had she done? She was alone in a motel room with a total stranger who was dishonest enough to cheat her in business, and she'd just knocked him clear into next week. He might very well decide to knock her clear into the one after that!

Her own trembling hand covered her lips, but he only straightened his shoulders, muscle by muscle, his anger held fiercely in check as he relaxed slowly, slowly. Without a word he retrieved his suitcase, opened the door, and paused, his eyes never leaving Lee's face.

"Just *who* looked through *whose* suitcase," he drawled, then added sarcastically, ". . . *lady?*"

He paused long enough to cause a warm flush to darken her cheeks before disappearing from the door, taking a smug grin with him.

In his wake Lee slammed the door so hard the mirror on the wall threatened to come crashing to the floor.

Chapter
TWO

A minute later Lee opened her suitcase only to stare, dismayed at its contents. *Oh no, not again,* she groaned. The distasteful magazine was still inside. It beckoned to Lee's seamier instincts. She began to close the suitcase, but a bit of royal blue peeked from beneath a folded dress shirt, making something forbidden and prurient tingle her insides. She crossed her arms nonchalantly over her waist, covertly glanced at the closed drapes, then slipped an innocent forefinger between the magazine pages, running it up and down thoughtfully several times before finally flipping the magazine open and crossing her arms tightly over her abdomen again.

She stared, mesmerized by the undeniably stunning

body stretched backward over a wide boulder on a riverbank. The skin was oiled, shimmering beneath drops of river spray with limbs laid open, hiding nothing. The model's eyes were closed, the expression on her face a combination of lust and fulfillment. The sultry, open lips were parted, the tongue peeking out between perfect teeth. Her long, scarlet nails rested against the dark triangle of femininity.

Lee swallowed, blushed, but turned the page. There followed more of the same. Skin and sin, she thought—exactly what one might expect of a man like Sam Brown. Still, she turned one more page.

The blood surged to her face, to her toes, to the backs of her knees, as she stared at the pornographic film clip from a current movie. Her stomach went weightless. Her chest felt tight, and the short hairs of her arms and thighs stood at attention. The man and woman were intimately entwined, limbs and teeth bared . . .

Sam Brown, you are disgusting! Abruptly she slapped the magazine shut, slammed the suitcase closed, and drew her hand back as if it had been singed, just as a knock sounded at her door.

Her head snapped up. She swallowed and pressed cool palms against hot cheeks before crossing the room and opening the door with much more control than she felt.

It was Sam Brown again. But this time his sport coat was gone and only one button held his shirt together at the waist. The shirttails were matted into a network of wrinkles, and in the deep V collar she again caught sight of the small silver cross set in turquoise. She dropped her eyes quickly from that bare chest only to find his feet bare too.

"Seems we've done it again," he ventured.

"Seems," she said crisply, not smiling.

She found it impossible to confront his eyes right after having confronted his girlie magazine. *Don't be silly, Walker, he's not a mind reader.* But still she felt that if he got a closer look, he'd know what she'd been doing when he knocked.

"I was getting set to go for a run when . . ." He flipped a palm up. "Same song, second verse." He peered past her to his suitcase which she knew was lying on the bed with the top closed but unzipped. Still she stood like a palace guard, holding the edge of the door with one hand, blocking his entrance.

"Listen, what I said before was inexcusable. I'd like to apologize," Sam Brown offered.

"I should think you would," Lee returned tightly, the image from the magazine still vivid in her mind.

He handed her the correct suitcase. "Is that any way to reply when I'm trying to bury the hatchet? The least you can do is be civil."

"All right. I . . . I shouldn't have slapped you either. I'm sorry. There, will that do?" But her voice was hard and cynical.

"Not quite." He pointed to his belongings. "I'd like my stuff back, too. I want to take a run and work off all my recent anger and frustration, but my sweats are in there."

He tilted a peace-offering grin at her, and she stepped back stiffly and motioned for him to come in and take what was his. She watched the wrinkles on his shirttails as he lifted the cover of the suitcase to check cursorily inside. The magazine lay on top. He studied it a moment, then spun to face her, a dark glower lowering his eyebrows.

"Look, just because a man buys a skin magazine doesn't make him a pervert."

"To each his own," she granted, but her tone was undeniably judgmental.

"The rag's got damn good interviews and movie reviews and—" Suddenly he turned sour-faced, slammed the top down, and zipped it with three jerks of the wrist. "I don't know why the hell I should justify myself to you. And anyway, why do you think you have the right to convict a man according to what you find in his suitcase?"

She sighed with overstrained patience. "Listen, do you mind? I've been in these clothes all day, and I'd like a bath and some supper. It's been a rough day."

"Fine . . . fine." He yanked the suitcase off the bed. "I'm leaving!"

She was waiting to close the door on his heels, but before she could, he wheeled to face her. Almost angrily he stated, "I *am* sorry for what I said. It was totally out of line, but so are you for not gracefully accepting my apology and letting me off the hook. Those eyes of yours are gl—"

"I said, apology accepted."

"Then how about if I buy you dinner and we can talk about . . . whatever? Anything but suitcases."

"No thank you, Mr. Brown. Not interested. I work for one insufferable sexist and can't help being around him an unavoidable amount of time each week, but beyond him, I'm careful about who I spend my time with."

Deep wrinkles appeared in his forehead as he scowled down at her. He looked ominous and ready to blow his cork again, but Lee held her ground, facing him squarely, one hand on the edge of the door. She was conscious again of how erect his posture was—even more so as he held his anger tightly in check—shoulders squared back, the inverted triangle of bare skin on his chest as taut as the head of a drum. He wore a tight-lipped expression as his dark eyes seemed to penetrate her for a long, threatening moment. Then he turned on a bare heel and stalked away.

With a shaky sigh of relief, Lee closed the door, leaned her forehead against it for a moment, then slipped the dead bolt home.

The tension of the day had keyed her up until her neck and shoulders felt stiff with fatigue. She leaned far back from the waist, slipped a thin hand to the nape of her neck, and kneaded. Eyes closed, hair trailing free, she wondered what had prompted Sam Brown to invite her to dinner. Then, recalling his choice of reading material, she thought she knew the answer.

Lee flopped tiredly on the bed, crossed her arms behind her head, and tried to rid her thoughts of Sam Brown. But his face intruded, as she'd first seen it at the bid letting when he was accepting handshakes—smiling, laughing, pleased with himself. She remembered the tiny wrinkles at the corners of his eyes and wondered how old he was? Mid-thirties? When he scowled, he looked older—and he'd done plenty of scowling today! But his look of displeasure also made his undeniably handsome face even more good looking.

She tossed a limp forearm over her brow. Handsome is as handsome does, she thought tiredly. She'd chalk this day up to experience and forget she had ever laid eyes on the man.

The face of Floyd A. Fat Thorpe nudged Brown's aside, and Lee wondered which of the two was more disturbing. Thorpe was going to be more offensive than ever after this fiasco. Especially since she had deliberately disobeyed orders and stayed the night in Denver. There were times when competing in a man's world didn't seem worth it. But she had to prove to herself she could . . . hadn't she? Hadn't she had to prove it not only to herself but also to everyone else who had helped wreck her life?

She fell into a fitful sleep with the faces of Thorpe and Brown mingling in a collage of other disturbing faces from her past—Joel's, the judge's . . .

AWAKENING with a start, Lee jerked her wrist up—seven thirty!—slid off the bed, and began undressing all in one motion.

She ran a tubful of water, took a quick refreshing bath, and cursed the thin motel towels and cheap soap that scarcely lathered. Drying herself, she stepped to the vanity, then tossed the towel aside while she rummaged for her brush and began smoothing her hair. It reached just below her shoulder blades—a coarse, black mane thicker than wild prairie grass, so thick she leaned sideways at the waist as if its weight made her list. She leaned in the other direction, then stood straight, watching her breast rise and fall rhythmically with each brush stroke.

Her hand stopped in midair, the brush momentarily

forgotten as she somberly assessed her naked reflection. Unbidden came the seductive pictures of the magazine and with them the vision of Sam Brown's face, his bare chest, his bare feet. She stared into her own dark eyes until her eyelids trembled, and she lowered her eyes. Her gaze moved down the long, lean neck to medium, pear-shaped breasts with dark nipples.

Hesitantly she brought the brush forward and ran the back of it around the outer edge of her right breast. The cool, yellow plastic was strangely smooth and welcome against her skin. She drifted it along the hollow beneath the breast, then up to the nipple. Tingles of remembrance came fluttering.

It had been a long time.

There were things a woman's body needed.

She closed her eyes as she turned the brush over, thinking of the whiskers on a firm jaw as she felt the light scrape of bristles along the side of her full breast, down her ribs, across her abdomen to the hollow of her hip.

A deep loneliness aroused memories of a past when her youthful dreams had consisted of rosy pictures of how life would turn out. Marriage, children, happy ever after. What had happened to all that? Why was she standing alone in a motel room in Denver, Colorado, remembering Joel Walker? He was married to someone else now, and, truth to tell, Lee no longer loved him. What she loved was the memory of those dreams she'd had when they'd first met, the wild want of each other's bodies that they'd thought was enough upon which to build a marriage. She ached for the time before all the mistakes had been made, before Jed and Matthew had been born.

Lee opened her eyes to find an empty, sad woman before her. A woman with pale stretch marks snaking from hip to abdomen as the only reminder of two pregnancies. She spread her fingers upon them and slumped against the vanity. Then she pushed herself erect and lifted her eyes. *Damn you, Lee, you promised yourself not to get bogged down in recriminations over what can't be changed!*

She took a firmer grip on the brush and began styling her hair, angrily brushing so hard her scalp hurt, dragging the heavy black mass around the back of her head and securing it just above and behind an ear in a heavy, smooth knot. Her skin was naturally bronze and needed neither foundation nor blush, but she accented her eyelids with silver shadow, curled her lashes, and applied eyeliner and mascara. Her lipstick was two-toned, a rich claret accented by white lipliner. She dashed a touch of perfume behind each ear and turned to get dressed.

She donned a pair of baggy white pants that tapered at the ankle above high-heeled wedges of canvas and rope, then a cavalry-style shirt of pale blue stripes that buttoned off center and had short puffed sleeves ending in ruffles at the elbow. A generous ruffled collar stood up around Lee's jaws, which she knew emphasized her long, graceful neck. Stepping to the mirror, again she added the ever-present feathers—this time hanging them in her ears, light blue wisps that dangled when she turned to retrieve her purse and head down to dinner.

The dining room was almost empty. Night had nearly fallen and the lights of Denver were glimmering on one by one beyond the windows. Lee paused in the doorway, peering into the dimness where unobtrusive music played quietly. In a far corner a gray-haired couple was sipping coffee. The only other occupied table in the room was taken by Sam Brown. He glanced up from a newspaper as Lee paused in the doorway. Their eyes met briefly before he turned expressionlessly back to his reading, angling the paper to catch the last fading light from the window beside him. Lee waited, feeling awkward and conspicuous as she studied the back of the cash register. At last a waitress led her to a seat.

Unfortunately it was in the middle of the floor and faced Sam Brown. Again he lifted his eyes. Again they returned laconically to his newspaper, and Lee felt more than ever like the lead act in a one-ring circus.

The waitress handed Lee a menu. "Kind of slow

tonight," the woman commented, her voice ringing like a clarion in the empty room.

"So I see."

"Can I get you anything from the bar?"

"Yes, a Smith and Kurn." Lee was conscious of Sam Brown's eyes directed her way again. "I know it's an after-dinner drink, but somehow I'm always too full then." She laughed nervously, damning herself for explaining, knowing she'd done it not for the waitress's benefit but for Sam Brown's. What did she care what he thought?

The waitress crossed to his table. She handed him a menu, and their voices also resounded clearly through the room.

"Something from the bar, sir?"

"An extra dry martini with pickled mushrooms, if you've got 'em."

My, aren't we fussy, Lee thought testily. Pickled mushrooms!

"We sure do," the waitress replied, and moved away to leave the room with nothing but that dim music which could scarcely fill the uncomfortable tension spinning between their two tables.

Lee searched her menu, immediately spotted what she wanted, but taking refuge behind the wide folder for a full five minutes until the waitress finally arrived with her drink gave Lee someplace else to focus her attention.

The chocolate-flavored drink was refreshing. Lee sipped and followed the waitress with her eyes as the uniformed back hid Sam Brown momentarily from view.

"We gave you a couple extra mushrooms. How's that?" came the pleasant question.

"Great, thank you." His deep voice reverberated in Lee's ears.

When the woman stepped back, Sam's eyes caught Lee's. Immediately she ducked to take a sip of her drink. The glass felt slippery in her hand. She dried her palm on her thigh, and applied herself to the menu again, ever so studiously, damning the waitress for walking off without asking if she was ready to order.

The woman returned at last with pencil and pad. So far Lee had managed to keep her eyes off the table by the window.

"Can I take your order now?"

Does a one-legged duck swim in a circle? Lee bit back the snippy retort and forcibly pasted a pleasant smile on her face. She attempted to speak softly, but the words came ringing off the walls like gunshots.

"I'll have ocean perch, no potato, and Thousand Island dressing on my salad."

"Would you like something in place of the potato?"

"Would I ever, but I'm being firm with myself

tonight." There followed a false laugh that Lee hardly recognized as her own while Brown's eyes probed once again. She suddenly felt as if she'd told him something personal that he had no right to know and damned herself for making the innocent comment.

He ordered prime rib, medium rare, baked potato with both butter and sour cream, the house dressing— without being told what it was, which for some reason irritated Lee, who ate in restaurants seldom enough not to be adventurous—and a cup of coffee.

This time when the waitress moved away, the eyes of the two diners met and hesitated on each other for a longer moment. Sam Brown now leaned back in his chair with lazy nonchalance, one shoulder angling lower than the other as he rested a negligent elbow on the table and touched the rim of his glass with five fingertips.

Lee sipped her drink and looked pointedly away, but the distracting memory of his magazine pictures came niggling again. She felt his eyes on her and for a moment had the disquieting impression he was stacking her up against his naked tootsies, wondering how she'd compare. To Lee's dismay, the memory of her stretch marks emblazoned itself across her mind.

"Did you get your bath?"

At the sound of his lazy question her eyes flew up, and she colored as if he'd just spoken an obscenity, then glanced quickly at the old couple in the corner. They were sipping silently, paying no attention whatsoever.

"Yes. Did you have your run?"

He smiled crookedly. "I tried, but the damn air in this city is so thin I felt like I was having a heart attack."

"A pity you didn't." She quirked one eyebrow and made the ice cubes bob with a poke of her finger.

"Still don't believe me, huh?"

She lifted her glass, eyed him over its rim, took a long, sweet sip, then slowly shook her head from side to side. "Uh-uh."

He shrugged indifferently, took a pull on his cocktail, and studied the view outside the window. The way he had one shoulder back farther than the other made the yellow knit shirt hug his chest like a wet buckskin. The front zipper was lowered several inches and the silver cross winked at Lee while she tried to pretend he wasn't there. But it was impossible when, a moment later, the old couple arose, paid their bill, and went away, leaving Lee and Sam the only two in the room.

The waitress returned, deposited their first courses, and disappeared again.

Lee dove into her salad like a sinner into a confessional. But every clink of fork upon bowl seemed amplified and disturbing. The sound of her own chewing seemed explosive in the room. She scarcely kept from wriggling in her chair while feeling Sam Brown's steady gaze resting on her in an increasingly distracting manner.

His voice split the quiet again. "You know this is ridiculous, don't you?"

She looked up to find him with hands resting idly next to his salad bowl.

"What is?" she managed.

"Sitting here like a couple of little kids who just had a fight over who broke the mud pie."

She couldn't think of a single sane reply. With an engaging grin he went on. "So, you're gonna stay in your yard and I'm gonna stay in mine, and we're going to glare at each other over the fence and be lonely and miserable while neither of us will make the first move."

She stared at him, gulped down what felt like an entire, unbroken head of lettuce, and said not a word.

"Can I bring my salad over there?" he asked finally, then added charmingly, "If I promise not to break your mud pie?"

The wisp of a smile threatened her lips and before she could control it she had chuckled, the sound bringing a wash of relief. "Yes, come ahead. It's awful sitting here trying not to look at you."

He and his salad and his pickled mushrooms were up and across the floor in three seconds. He settled himself at her table, gave her an audacious grin, and declared, "There, that's better," then dug into his lettuce with gusto.

She had called him a liar, a cheat, and a pervert. What possible course of conversation could successfully follow that? she wondered uneasily. To her relief, he came up with one.

"I have to admit, you're the first lady estimator I've ever seen."

"I'm the first lady estimator *I've* ever seen," she admitted.

The deep lines on either side of his mouth dented in. "How long have you been one?"

"I began in the business three years ago and have been an estimator for a little over a year."

"Why?"

Her eyebrows curled in puzzlement. "What do you mean, why?"

"Why choose a career in a tough business like this that's traditionally been dominated by men?"

"Because it pays well."

He accepted that with a nod of the head. "You work for old Floyd Thorpe, huh?"

"Yes, I'm sorry to say I do."

"He's a hell-raiser that one—a real shyster."

Startled, she looked into his dark eyes. "You know him?"

"He's been around Kansas City a long time. Everybody there knows old Floyd. It's his kind that give construction companies a bad reputation. He's as crooked as a dog's hind leg."

"But he knows how to make money so he's excused, right?" she questioned sarcastically.

Refusing to rise to the bait, Sam asked, "If you dislike him so much, why work for him?"

"With the construction industry tied directly to new-home starts, need you ask?"

He wiped his mouth on a napkin. "No, I guess there aren't a lot of job openings right now, are there?"

She poked at the fleshy wedge of tomato in her bowl as if it were Thorpe's fat belly. "The only opening I've seen lately is the one between Floyd Thorpe's front teeth when he spits his slimy tobacco juice at my feet."

Brown laughed appreciatively, prompting Lee to look up with a devilish expression on her face. "Can I share a very private joke with you? One that's exceedingly irreverent?"

"I love irreverent jokes."

Lee sucked on her bottom lip, then confessed, "Privately, when I'm disgusted with my boss, which I usually am, I call him by his initials."

"Which are?"

"F.A.T." Brown rocked back in his chair and

laughed while she continued, "He doesn't like it generally known what his middle initial is. Maybe that's why I take such pleasure in including it."

The fine white lines about Brown's eyes disappeared as he crinkled a smile and watched as she jabbed repeatedly at the tomato. His eyes passed over high, wide cheekbones, the proud, straight nose, the black straight hair caught behind her ear, in a plump, smooth bun, the copper skin and near-black eyes.

"You're Indian, right?"

Her eyes flashed up defiantly, and the feathers swung against her jaws. "One quarter Cherokee. He never lets me forget it."

Brown glanced at the feathers but withheld comment. "What you're saying is old Fat knows which side his bread is buttered on, huh?"

"Exactly. He's asked me no less than five times to accept the *honorary* title of vice-president."

"Let me guess." Brown leaned forward. "That would qualify him as a minority contractor, right?"

She grinned ruefully. "*And* make him eligible to bid any and all Minority Business Enterprise jobs the federal government lets, either as prime contractor or subcontractor. As you know, they seem to be the best bet going right now."

He studied her from beneath black brows shaped like boomerangs. "I take it you've declined the vice-presidency."

"With great relish."

Again Sam Brown leaned back in his chair and laughed richly. "There are a few contractors in the Kansas City area who'd grin from ear to ear to hear somebody put one over on F.A. after all the times he's pulled underhanded deals."

"I'd grin wider myself if it weren't for the increase in pay I'm turning down just to make Fat Thorpe eat crow."

"Or—more aptly—Cherokee?" Sam quipped, watching her closely.

She chuckled and her dark eyes sparkled momentarily before a pensive look overcame them. She nudged a few remaining pieces of lettuce around her salad bowl and folded her knuckles beneath her chin. She braced one elbow on the table, rested her other forearm against the edge of the table, and stroked the damp sides of her cold glass. "You know," she mused to the ice cubes in the empty tumbler, "there are some things my pride just won't let me do. Not even for money."

"But I thought you said money was why you took the job."

"It was. But I earn enough to support myself now. That's all I need."

She saw his eyes drop to the hand toying with the glass. It bore only a large oval turquoise in a sterling silver setting.

"You're not married?" he asked.

His eyes moved higher, met hers, and her fingers stopped stroking the damp glass.

"No," she answered tersely, realizing she should qualify the answer, then disregarded her conscience, thinking she owed this man nothing. They were simply sharing a table—two strangers in a lonely city away from home.

Their main course arrived, and Sam Brown changed the subject. "I take it *the Fat* is going to hit the fan when he hears you lost the bid, huh?"

Lee looked up, chuckled appreciatively, and noted, "You *do* have an irreverent sense of humor, don't you? He's always hitting the fan over one thing or another. It's a way of life with him. If it's not over losing the bid, it'll be over me staying overnight on his precious company credit card, which he warned me not to do."

"But you're doing it anyway?" A frown tilted his brows.

"It was either that or get into Kansas City in the middle of the night after missing the six P.M. flight out of here. After the day I've put in, I wasn't about to spend half the night in a plane."

"All because I had your suitcase, right?"

She met his eyes, but only shrugged and returned to her dinner.

The waitress brought coffee, interrupting them

momentarily. When they were alone again, Lee studied Sam thoughtfully and asked, "If you've been around the K.C. area long enough to know about the questionable business practices of my illustrious boss, why haven't we met before?"

"Probably because we've been primarily involved with plumbing contracting and only recently decided to expand into sewer and water work."

"We?" she asked curiously. "Who's the other Brown in Brown and Brown?"

"It was my dad. He was the one who knew every contractor's secrets around town. He was in the contracting business for years."

"Was?"

"He died four years ago," Sam stated unemotionally, cutting into his prime rib.

"I . . . I'm sorry."

He looked up brightly. "Oh, don't be. My father had a hell of a good life, did everything he ever wanted to do, died a happy man . . . on a golf course, no less, on the sixth tee." His brown eyes twinkled. "That sixth tee always did give him trouble."

Even though Sam Brown pronounced all this with no apparent sadness, Lee felt awkward sharing his private history this way when she scarcely knew him. But he went on. "He was a hard-drinking, hard-working Norwegian—"

"A Norwegian named *Brown?*"

"Comes from Brunvedt, somewhere back along the line."

"I'm sorry . . . I interrupted."

"Well as I said, he was a hard-headed Norwegian, and when I say he did everything he wanted, that included disobeying doctor's orders. He'd had a small stroke and was given orders to take it easy for a few months, but when a stubborn Norwegian takes it into his head he's going to go golfing, there's no stopping him."

Lee found she was enjoying Sam Brown's company immensely by now and surprised even herself by replying, "And when a stubborn Norwegian takes it into his head that he's going to go to dinner with a woman, there's no stopping him either, is there?"

Sam angled a smile at the knot of hair behind her ear, then at her eyes, and finally her lips. It occurred to Lee that he looked nothing whatever like any Norwegian she'd ever met. His hair was a rich chestnut color, his eyes and skin so dark they seemed to reflect her very face as he reached blindly for his coffee cup and—without taking his eyes from her—teased, "Well, it wasn't so painful after all, was it?"

She wished she could answer otherwise, but she found it impossible. "Admittedly, no it wasn't."

"Maybe we can do it again sometime in Kansas City."

For a moment she was tempted, but recalling the less estimable aspects of his personality, she warned, "Don't plan on it. Not unless *I've* won the bid."

"Mmm . . ." He lifted his coffee. Devilish eyes sparkled above the cup. "Might be worth fixing the bid in your favor next time."

"I have no doubt you'd do it." She studied him for some time, then admitted, "I have a habit of coining titles for people I meet. You know what I've dubbed you?"

"What?"

Their eyes tangled in a delightful duel of wits.

"The Honorable Sam Brown."

"Hey, I like that . . . that's clever."

"And pure, unvarnished sarcasm. Brown, you're a completely dishonorable scoundrel, and I don't know why I'm sitting at this table with you right now."

He tipped his chair back until it balanced on two legs. "Because you wanted to find out if I'm as perverted as my reading material led you to suspect. They say every woman is attracted to the wrong kind of man at least once in her life. Who knows? Maybe I'm it for you."

"Then again maybe you're not." She tipped her head and studied him closely. He was a highly delicious looking male specimen—she'd grant him that. And his nasty sense of humor didn't hurt a bit. But Lee reminded herself again that he wasn't the sort

45

with whom she should be bantering about sexually provocative things. Conversations such as this provoked vibrations that said much more than the mere words, and she was by no means ready for such vibrations again. Her wounds hadn't healed from the last disastrous relationship. But even while she chided herself for indulging in such give-and-take, Sam's eyes were steady on her as his chair came down on all fours. He leaned crossed arms on the table edge, and pitched slightly toward her.

"Tell me," he said, his voice gone low and intimate. "What'd you think of the one stretched out on the rock beside the river?"

Damned if she was going to look like some nilly-witted teenager caught peeping at African breasts in *National Geographic!* Lee looked Brown smack in the eye and replied levelly, "The photographer must have missed oiling the inner side of her right calf. The water didn't bead up there."

Sam Brown rewarded her with a full-throated, appreciative peal of laughter while Lee scolded herself for her own precociousness. A moment later he had flung his soiled napkin on the table, picked up the check and was standing behind her chair, waiting to pull it back. But before he did, he leaned close and, just beside an aqua feather, said, "Chief Sitting Bull would have excommunicated you from the tribe if he'd ha . . . ha . . ." He turned away just in time. *"Aaa-chooo!"*

She glanced over her shoulder with a cheeky grin. "My goodness, Brown, it looks like you're allergic to me. Don't get so close next time."

He was rubbing his nose with a handkerchief. "It's that perfume you're wearing."

"My apologies." She grinned, not feeling the least bit of contrition.

It's just as well, she thought. She had no business being with him in the first place. But still she had to smile, for on the way back to their rooms he sneezed three more times, and by the time they reached her door he was giving her a good six-foot clearance.

Chapter
THREE

FLOYD A. Thorpe kept his office like he kept his teeth—brown around the edges. Rolls of plans, soil samples, drill bits, cast-iron pipe fittings, test plugs, incoming mail, hydrant wrenches, and used coffee cups created a random scattering of litter that was rarely cleared or dusted, for F.A. raised particular hell if anyone monkeyed with his "filing system." The room had an unpleasant smell, a mixture of rancid chewing tobacco, dust, stale alcohol, tar, and dried clay, topped off with the peculiar smell of cast iron. When Lee had taken the job at Thorpe Construction, F.A. had been in the middle of one of his sporadic drying-out periods, during which he became less abusive and more reasonable. The office had been cleaner, and so had he.

But he'd been off the wagon for months now. His nose shone like a beacon, and his cheeks wore the mottled red puffiness of the serious drinker. It was all Lee could do to face him the following morning across the junk on his desk.

"He what!" bellowed F.A.

Lee took a step backward. Thorpe's breakfast Manhattan was offensive the second time around.

"He got my suitcase by mistake, found the bid inside, and turned it in along with his own."

"And took the goddam job away from you like candy from a baby!" F.A. fumed and paced, then picked up a coffee can and spit into it. Lee studied a piece of P.V.C. pipe on a littered file cabinet behind him rather than observe the distasteful sight of his brown spume. "By a measly four thousand dollars!" F.A. whammed his fist into the center of the desk, lifting dust and making the telephone dance. He dropped into his desk chair and glowered at Lee, then turned suddenly pensive. "That's old Wayne Brown's kid, isn't it? Mmm . . . appears the kid's got more brains than his old man." Thorpe's eyes narrowed shrewdly, and he chuckled deep in his throat. Then he turned his beady eyes on Lee again. "I hope you learned your lesson from this. Everybody's out to screw everybody else in this world, and Sam Brown proved it!" With a quick shift of weight, he leaned back in his chair. "You thought any more about that vice-presidency I offered you?"

"Sorry, I prefer estimating."

Again he banged his fist on the desk. "Damn it, Walker, I put up with a lot from you, carrying your bids in a suitcase like some green recruit, then picking up the wrong damn one at the other end of the line and losing me a job worth over four million bucks! How long do you think I'm going to put up with screw-ups like this! I want your name on them corporation papers. It's the least you can do after the mess you made out of this Denver bid."

"I'm sorry about losing the suitcase, but the rest of it wasn't my fault. If Sam Brown checked my bid against his, he wouldn't admit it."

"Why, hell no, who would?" F.A.'s pot belly was so hard it scarcely depressed when he crossed his hands on it. "Tell you what, girlie. I'll give you till Friday to think it over. Either you help me out with this here minority business thing and agree to become vice-president, or you can find yourself someplace else to work. You're costin' me money, and unless you help me make a little of it back, I got no use for you."

Back in her own neat office, Lee strode angrily to her chair, deposited herself in it with great vexation, cursed under her breath, and considered marching back in there and telling F.A.T. where to put his vice-presidency *and* his tobacco cud! There'd be nothing so sweet as to walk out there and show that fat, smelly boar she didn't need his precious job or his calculating little mind one moment longer.

But the bitter truth was, she did.

She had no husband across town bringing in a paycheck from another job to support her. She was self-reliant now and needed a weekly salary to survive. Sam Brown had been right when he'd summed up the estimator's job market right now—there was none! Two years ago, before the recession had gripped the country, Kansas City and its surrounding suburbs had had perhaps twenty more general contractors than it did now. Now the industry grapevine buzzed constantly with news of this one or that one on the verge of folding, and they all held their breaths, hoping the next one to go under wouldn't be themselves.

The phone interrupted Lee's reverie. She punched line one and answered, "Lee Walker."

"You made it back."

The voice surprised Lee.

"Brown, is that you?"

"That's right, the Honorable Sam Brown. I looked for you on my flight. Thought we might sit together and share my magazine."

She didn't feel in the least like smiling but couldn't

help it. Damn the man, making her laugh when he'd been the initial cause of the altercation she'd just had with Thorpe!

"Oh, you did, huh? I took an earlier flight. I've been back since ten o'clock."

A brief pause, then, "How did Thorpe take the news?"

She laughed, a single mirthless huff. "Need you ask?"

"Well, you win a few and you lose a few. He should know that by now."

"That isn't even remotely funny, Brown. Not after what you did to me! He came down on me like a tent when the circus is over, and what really irritates me is that Fat Thorpe actually seems to admire you for your duplicity. His exact words were, 'The kid's got more brains than his old man.' It appears you're two peas in a pod, you and my boss."

His unconcerned laughter came over the wire. "We're both a couple of degenerates, is that it?"

"That's it," she agreed.

"Well, how would you like a chance to try your hand at reforming me . . . say over dinner Friday night?"

Lee came close to sputtering, the dressing down she'd just taken from F.A. still burning beneath her collar. "Dinner! What, again? And ruin my reputation around this town by being seen with a known pervert? I told you, Brown, I don't know why I ate with you the first time!"

"I'll take you to the American Restaurant," he bribed.

The American! Lee was suddenly crestfallen and undeniably tempted. The American Restaurant at the Crown Center was the *crème de la crème* of eateries in the Kansas City area.

"Brown, that's a dirty, rotten low blow, and you know it."

"I know," he agreed mirthfully, a smile in his voice.

"I told you, not until *I'm* the low bidder, and right now I'm not, as you well know." *The American Restaurant,* she thought woefully, kissing the chance good-bye.

"Okay, Cherokee, but I'll hold you to it . . . when you're low bidder."

"Ch . . ." Now Lee did sputter! "Ch . . . Cherokee! Brown, don't you ever call me that ag . . . Brown?" She clicked the disconnect button. "Brown!"

But he'd hung up. Then she did too, slamming the receiver down so hard it jumped back off the cradle. "Cherokee!" she spit out crossing her arms and glaring at the instrument guilty of carrying his damn sexy, teasing voice to her when she was in no mood to be manipulated by a smooth talker like him.

How dare he call her Cherokee when . . . when . . .

But a moment later her lips betrayed her and she found herself grinning at the phone. It was the last time she grinned that day.

Things went from bad to worse. Fat Thorpe pounded in and out, cussing like a marine and demanding test borings on jobs Lee knew were too wet to even consider bidding; ordering installation of inferior quality pipe they'd had trouble with before; demanding last minute changes in a bid she'd all but finished. He became more overbearing and demanding as the day passed. Lee required all her teeth-gritting strength to maintain her composure.

By the time she left the office, her nerves were at the breaking point. She arrived at her townhouse tired, angry, and depressed. In the front foyer she stripped off her shoes and pantyhose and left them lying in a heap. There was something about bare feet that seemed to take the stress off her head.

In the rear-facing kitchen she reached unseeingly into the refrigerator for a peach, and sank her teeth into it while roaming over to the sliding glass door and staring at her tiny private patio, fantasizing about calling the Human Rights Commission to complain that she was being discriminated against. But what could the complaint be? That Old Fat wanted to make her vice-president and give her a raise but she was declining the offer? There was nothing illegal about Thorpe's ploy to make his firm eligible as a minority contractor. It was only unethical! And Lee adamantly refused to be his patsy in the scheme.

She prowled the living room, heaping curses on Old Fat's fat head! Spying the newspaper, she checked the *Kansas City Star,* but as she'd suspected, no one wanted estimators. *The Construction Bulletin* turned up nothing more, and Lee's depression grew.

Sitting on the floor, her back to the sofa, she crossed her arms over upraised knees and rested her forehead there. The peach pit grew warm and slippery in her hand. She raised her head wearily and propped her chin on an arm, studying the precision pleats of the off-white custom-made draperies she was still paying off in monthly installments.

She'd worked so hard to get this place. She brushed a hand over the thick nap of the rich, rust carpet. She'd bought the townhouse only six months ago, and though she had a long way to go before it was completely decorated, she loved the furniture she'd managed to buy so far. She had modest dreams of adding decorator items piece by piece, of completing the finishing touches as she could afford them.

She sighed, slunk low onto her tailbone, and caught the nape of her neck on the cushion of the tuxedo sofa, which was covered with an arresting Mayan design of rich, deep earth tones, its soft depths strewn with plump matching cushions. Lee's eyes moved to the spots where she wanted side chairs.

But the room made her suddenly feel lonelier than ever. She studied the plants in the baskets, willing them to grow faster and fill up the extra space. Her eyes moved next to the only other item the room possessed—a loosely strung God's-eye on the wall behind the sofa, its rust, brown and ecru yarns so inexpertly stretched around the crossed dowels, that there could be no question it had been done by a child's hand.

Yes, the room was decidedly bare and lonely, but it was a beginning, and if she lost her job, she would lose this too.

Dejected, she wandered back to the kitchen, threw out the peach pit, rinsed off her hands and opened the refrigerator again only to find herself, some two minutes later, still staring into its almost empty space, remembering a day when she had shuffled and rearranged, trying to make room for family leftovers.

She closed the door on her memories, wishing the judge could see now what she'd made of herself since she'd faced him in court. Carrying a quart of milk onto the patio, she sank into a webbed lounge chair and drank the remainder of her supper right out of the red and white carton, too dispirited to care if it was in a glass or not.

It was much later when she finally plodded upstairs. The second floor of the townhouse had two bedrooms and a bath. As she neared the door of the smaller room, she slowed. Stopping, she reached inside and switched on the light. A pair of twin beds with heavy pine headboards took up the far wall. Between them stood a matching chest of drawers whose rich, dark wood looked richer against the bright scarlet carpet, but whose top was bare—nothing there but a lamp and an unopened box of paper tissues. Still, the room was completely decorated. The bedspreads and draperies were crisp and new, with an all-over design of NFL insignias in a blaze of basic colors. On the wall beside one bed hung two Kansas City Chiefs pennants.

Lee studied the room sullenly, biting back tears that stung her eyes, feeling again the frustrating sense of unfairness that she could never shake at the thought of the boys.

She counted the days.

A brown and white cat padded silently into the room and preened his fur against Lee's ankle.

"Oh, P. Ewing, you've been on the bed again, haven't you?"

Lee looked down, watched the cat move sinuously against her, then crossed to one of the beds to plump its pillow and smooth the spread. On her way out she scooped up the cat, buried her face in his fur, and reached for the light switch. But she paused in the doorway and turned, assessing the silent room once more. "Oh, P. Ewing, what if I lose my job?" she lamented. "I'll have to give up this place."

* * *

O N Friday morning Lee was working on a bid for a simple sewer and water installation in Overland Park, which would service an area where a shopping mall was to be built. The bid letting was scheduled for two that afternoon. These last few hours were always the worst. The phone constantly jangled with calls from salesmen giving last minute quotes on materials, from reinforced concrete pipe to catch basin castings. She'd just received a price quote on sod replacement which was several cents under the previous low bidder and was recomputing the labor subcontract cost when the phone rang. Preoccupied, fingers still flying over the calculator buttons, Lee reached unconsciously for the receiver, cradling it between shoulder and ear as her eyes continued scanning a column of numbers.

A moment later she realized she'd picked up a call meant for F.A. A smooth, masculine voice was saying, ". . . can come to terms on that twelve-inch reinforced concrete pipe we've had laying around the yard. The flaws are in the reinforcing, not in the concrete itself, so it'd be mighty tough to detect."

F.A. chuckled, then returned in a silky tone, "And we'll split the difference right up the middle?"

Horrified, Lee jerked the receiver away from her ear, clutching it in white knuckles, realizing she should have hung up the moment she'd identified the call as someone else's. But it had happened so fast! She rested the receiver on her job sheets and stared at the lighted button on the face of the phone, waiting, digesting what she'd heard. With each passing second her disgust grew. She'd heard it said many times that F.A. knew every dishonest trick in the book and wasn't afraid to use them. But she'd never had proof before. Using substandard materials, price fixing, collusion, buying off the competition before bids—there were countless deceits it was possible to practice. Some were illegal, some merely dishonest. But either way, until now it had been no more than hearsay.

The light blinked off, and Lee slipped the receiver silently back in place.

She was still sitting there in a turmoil when F.A. rounded the doorway into her office. This morning the gnawed stub of an unlit cigar was clenched in his teeth.

"Whoever you got to supply the twelve-inch reinforced concrete pipe on that Overland Park job, we won't be goin' with them. Gonna get that pipe from Jacobi."

"Oh?" Lee retorted coldly.

"Yeah, you can figure it at twelve-fifty a foot, materials only."

"And what margin of profit are you working on at twelve dollars and fifty cents a foot?"

His beady little eyes narrowed on her like laser beams. The cigar stub shifted to the opposite corner of his mouth. "Never mind, just figure it at twelve-fifty a foot."

Lee erupted from her chair. "No, *you* figure it at twelve-fifty a foot!"

"Me! That bid's due at two o'clock this afternoon and—"

"And it won't be turned in by me, not with flawed pipe from Jacobi figured into it!"

His sausagelike fingers slowly extracted the wet cigar from his lips. "So, Little Miss Big Ears has been listening in on somebody else's phone conversations, huh?"

"Yes, I heard you and Jacobi on the phone just now, but it was entirely unintentional. As a matter of fact, I only heard about ten seconds worth of the conversation."

"But it was enough to give you a sudden case of *morality,* is that it?" He managed to make the word sound quite dirty.

Lee's insides quivered. She pressed a thigh against the edge of her desk to steady the nerves that wanted to fly in six directions. "It's dishonest!"

Thorpe shifted till his shoulder leaned toward her

like a baseball pitcher studying signals from a catcher. He jabbed the cigar butt before her nose. "It's profit. And don't you forget it!"

"Profit earned at the expense of the taxpayer . . . *and* the environment, I might add!"

"Well, bye-dee-ho!" F.A. ran his eyes around the walls of her office as if searching for something. "Too bad we ain't got a stake around here so you can tie yourself to it and strike a match," he sneered.

Lee was already jerking her desk drawers open, setting her briefcase on the chair, snapping it open, separating personal items from company items.

"I refuse to be a party to your . . . your flawed materials or your scheme to qualify as a minority contractor. Why, I wouldn't be an officer of this company if Geronimo himself were president!" She piled up address book, legal pads, and portfolios in the center of her desk, each sharp slap like an exclamation point in the room.

"Geronimo wouldn't have the smarts it takes to run a business like this and turn a profit during a year as tough as this's been! In one phone call I clear a smooth ten thousand. Now what the hell kind of fool would turn down money like that?"

Lee stopped packing, rested her knuckles on the desktop, and skewered him with a feral glare. "And nobody's the wiser when five years from now the pipe breaks and untreated sewage infiltrates somebody's water supply, or . . . or runs into the Missouri River or—"

"A regular Albert Schweitzer, ain't you? Well, supposing I was to cut you in on a share of my take on this little deal, and you make me a minority contractor after all. Would a few thousand ease your conscience any?"

His cocky, self-assured belief that anybody could be bought off only sickened Lee all the more. She was suddenly very, very sure she was doing what should have been done months ago. Suddenly her anger disappeared and a renewed sense of well-being swept over her. Her lips relaxed; her voice quieted.

"Suppose it would. And what would be the next unethical thing you'd ask me to do? And the next? And how long would it be before you asked me to make the transition from unethical to illegal? You know, F.A., it isn't just the money—it's something much deeper than that. It's something born in an Indian that can't be programmed out. Call it elemental respect for the earth . . . or whatever you like. It's part of the reason I do what I do. I can't stop development or urban sprawl. But I *can* do my part to see that it doesn't completely annihilate the environment. I agree with you, Geronimo probably wouldn't be a rich man if he ran this company or one like it, but he'd probably rather drink clean water than deposit ten thousand dollars in the bank." Lee scanned her cleared desktop, then chuckled and smiled at F.A. "Come to think of it, Indians never were famous for saving for a rainy day, were they?"

Lee's belongings were piled on the desk and the chair. She snapped the briefcase shut, picked up an armful of notebooks and folders, and turned toward the door.

"But what about that bid for this afternoon?" Thorpe squawked.

"Finish it yourself."

"Girlie, you walk out of here, you give up unemployment checks, cause I ain't claimin' I laid you off. And don't look for no recommendations from—"

The outside door cut off his spate. As if his recommendation was worth anything at all around this town, Lee thought, as she headed toward the parking lot.

Her red Ford Pinto was parked right beside Thorpe's long, sleek Diamond Jubilee Mark V. The navy blue sedan was covered with a fine layer of dust, as if he'd recently driven through a jobsite. Lee dumped her load on the back seat of the Pinto, then straightened and studied Floyd's dusty status symbol. Imbedded in the glass of the opera window—still intact—was the illustrious but now lusterless diamond.

With a sardonic smile Lee leaned over, breathed on it, lifted an elbow, and polished it carefully. She stepped back to survey it critically, nodded once, then clambered into her Pinto and drove away.

* * *

BUT her cocky attitude had totally disappeared when, three days later, she'd turned up absolutely nothing resembling a job opening. As she paced the floor, she told herself she'd done the only thing possible. She was reviewing the miles she'd put on both her car and her feet during the past three days when her phone rang. Picking it up from the kitchen counter, the Honorable Sam Brown's was the last voice on earth she expected at the other end of the line.

"Who the hell are you trying to hide from?" he said without preamble.

"What?"

"I've been trying to get your damn phone number for three days!"

"And just who might this be?" she queried with undisguised sugar in every syllable.

"This, my little Indian, is the Honorable Sam Brown speaking. Just why in hell aren't you listed in the phone book?"

"Because I'm divorced and I don't want any obscene phone calls. And why didn't you just call Thorpe Construction for my number?"

"I did, but it seems Fat Floyd developed a conscience—belatedly, I might add—and declined to give out confidential information."

"Why that fat rat!"

"My sentiments exactly."

"So how did you get it?"

"I spent sixty-five bucks taking out a dumb red-head and buying her dinner, then plying her with a German wine because she works for Ma Bell."

Lee was dumbfounded. "You *whaaaat?*"

"And all she was good for at the end of the evening was a chaste good night kiss." He chuckled wickedly.

"I told you, Brown, I don't accept obscene phone calls."

"Too bad, cause the redhead finally gave over—your phone number, of course."

"Brown, you scheming weasel, are you saying you bribed the girl to get my unlisted number?"

"Call it what you will . . . I got it, didn't I?"

"For what?"

"I heard Fat Floyd gave you the ax."

"Well, you heard wrong. I quit."

"Bully for you. Have you got another job yet?"

"Are you kidding? I've been beatin' feet from one end of this town to the other, but it's hopeless."

"Listen, I've got a proposition for you."

"I'll just bet you do, but I'm not that desperate yet. If it's the same one you offered the redhead on her doorstep, keep it."

"You're the most suspicious woman I ever paid sixty-five dollars for, you know that?"

"And I'll bet there've been plenty, right?"

"Quit your goading, Cherokee, this is legitimate business. I'd like to talk to you about coming to work for me."

"You wh—"

"But I won't discuss it on the phone. I never carry out an interview by phone, only face to face. Are you busy tomorrow night?"

"Brown, you're crazy!"

He went on as if she hadn't spoken. "I'm busy all day tomorrow, including lunch, or we could get together then. But I'll be free by—oh, say, four thirty. Why don't we meet someplace for cocktails and discuss it then?"

"Brown, I can't come to work for you. It'd be like jumping from the pot into the fire!"

"Listen, I'd like to stay and listen to all this sweet talk, but I'm on the run as it is. Meet me at fifty-three oh-one State Line Road and we'll discuss it sensibly. Fifty-three oh-one State Line . . . got that?"

"Sam Brown, I don't trust you. What makes you think—"

But he'd done it again.

"Brown? . . . Brown, come back here!"

He'd left her with a dead receiver, and before the address escaped Lee's head, she was scrambling for a pencil.

Chapter
FOUR

FIVE-THREE-OH-ONE State Line Road turned out to be a place so grandiose that Lee drove right past it two times without even considering it might be the right spot. It was magnificent. Perched imposingly at the crest of a hill, it dominated the view with a white facade that reminded Lee of an antebellum mansion. Staring up at it, she fully expected Scarlett O'Hara to come flouncing through the door. The horseshoe-shaped drive rose toward the building, encircling a curve of lush green grass and an imposing flower bed that provided the only clue to the building's identity—a stunning "C C" formed by vibrant red and white geraniums.

It appeared to be a country club, backing up to

Ward Parkway, perhaps the most prestigious street in town with its countless fountains and mansions built by the oldest, moneyed forefathers. Lee had no doubt whatever that the place had a private membership of the highest echelon.

And Sam Brown was a member of *this?*

Leaving the car, Lee critically swished a hand over her skirt—thank God she hadn't worn slacks! Even the dress seemed less than adequate, for it was only a casual two-piece cotton outfit of brown and white stripes, the top an athletic looking slipover with ribbed waist, cap sleeves, and boatneck styling.

The shrubbery around the entrance looked artificial, it was so perfectly manicured. Tubs of potted flowers blossomed in colorful profusion on either side of the steps. Halting just short of them, Lee pulled a wand of lipgloss from her purse, checked her face in a tiny mirror, and applied a gleaming line of amber to her lips. Clamping her clutch bag beneath an elbow, she entered the "C C"—whatever it was!

She found herself in a vast room with high, wide windows off to the left through which the afternoon sun lit a tasteful grouping of antique furniture. A fireplace flanked the conversation area while enormous bouquets of silk flowers made the elegant old furniture appear even more valuable.

A discreet voice made her jump. "Ms. Walker?"

Lee turned to find a faultlessly dressed woman

smiling at her from behind rimless glasses with a chain dangling from their bows. The woman looked like she might very well own the place.

"Yes?" a puzzled Lee returned.

"Ah, I thought so by Mr. Brown's description of you. You'll find him downstairs in the lounge. Just follow that stairway around and it'll take you right to him." With a graceful wave of her hand, the woman withdrew.

Lee followed the stairs as directed to find herself in a low-ceilinged bar with reduced lighting. She scarcely had time to note that Sam Brown wasn't there before a smiling black man in formal waiter's attire approached to ask, much as the woman upstairs had, "Ms. Walker?"

"Yes."

"Mr. Brown is waiting for you in the lounge, if you'll follow me."

He led the way to another elegant room much like the one upstairs, only smaller and more intimate, with soft lighting from tasteful table lamps. Again there was a fireplace on the far wall and a scattering of plush furniture placed in cozy groupings. Sam Brown stretched his tall frame up from one of the antique wing chairs flanking the fireplace.

"Here she is, Mr. Brown," the waiter announced.

"Thank you, Walter." To Lee, Sam said, "I see you found the place all right."

"Not without some trouble," she admitted, taking in his dark gaze as it swept her hair and face.

"Will the lady be wanting a cocktail?" Walter inquired.

"Yes, a Smith and Kurn," Brown answered before the waiter left them discreetly alone. Then he turned to Lee, gesturing. "Sit down, Ms. Walker."

In spite of herself she was pleased that he'd remembered her drink preference, and it tempered her voice as she chided, "Don't you Ms. Walker me, Sam Brown. Why didn't you warn me what kind of place this was?"

She perched on a Chippendale love seat while Brown chose the spot beside her rather than the chair he'd been occupying earlier. He turned sideways, lifting a knee partially onto the cushioned seat and resting his arm along its back. He scrutinized her with a half smile.

"Why? You look great, Cherokee."

"And don't call me Cherokee." She looked around furtively to see if anyone had heard, but they were alone in the lounge.

"If Ms. Walker and Cherokee are both out, what should I call you?"

She didn't know. "Try Lee," she finally suggested.

"All right, Lee, you had some trouble finding the place?"

"Trouble! I drove right past it two times and never even gave it a glance. What is it, anyway?"

"It's the Carriage Club."

"And you're a member, I take it."

"Aha." He reached for his cocktail from an oval table in front of the sofa. The entire grouping, including the pair of wing chairs, faced the fireplace, ensconcing them in a private circle of their own.

She turned her eyes to the coffee table. In addition to a bouquet of freshly cut spider mums and carnations, it held a silver bowl of macadamia nuts. Her gaze moved over richly papered walls to the polished andirons and screen in the fireplace. Slowly Lee's eyes traveled back to Sam Brown to find him studying her.

"Is this supposed to change my opinion of . . . the decadent rich?" she asked.

He shrugged, but his grin remained.

Just then Walter returned with her Smith and Kurn, set it on the table, and inquired, "And will there be anything else for you, Mr. Brown?"

"Another of the same."

As soon as Walter had faded away, Lee couldn't resist querying, "What? Aren't you going to ask for pickled mushrooms?"

"The decadent rich don't need to ask. Walter knows exactly how I prefer my drinks."

"So . . . you're a member of good standing?"

His only answer was the continued amiable expression on his face, and against her will, Lee Walker *was* thoroughly impressed.

"I came here to talk business, Mr. Brown," she said.

"Of course." He leaned forward slightly. "Unlike most of the contracting firms in this city, mine has had a good year. The plumbing half of the firm has sustained the sewer and water half until it can get on its feet. All I need is one good estimator."

"And what makes you think I'm good?"

"You damn near beat me out of that Denver job, and you did beat out an impressive lineup of competition. I want anybody who can do that working for me, not against me."

"I did beat you out, and you know it," she accused in a soft voice.

"Are we going to beat that old dead horse again?"

"I couldn't resist."

His brown eyes crinkled. Distracted, she reached for some nuts.

"Are you interested in the job offer?"

She didn't want to be, but—damn his dark eyes!—she was. Walter intruded momentarily to lean low with a silver tray, and even over his back Lee could feel Sam Brown's eyes following her hand as she lifted the nuts to her mouth, then licked away the salt that caught on her glossy lipstick.

She raised her eyes to confront him head on. "I want you to know right off the bat—I don't do anybody's dirty work. I bid 'em straight and fair."

"I'll pay you forty thousand a year, plus a company car and all the usual fringe benefits—profit sharing, insurance, use of a company credit card."

While shock waves catapulted through Lee, she watched Sam lazily stir his drink, then lift a red plastic saber upon which four pickled mushrooms were skewered. His sparkling teeth slipped the first mushroom into his mouth, and his jaws began moving while hers went slack.

"Forty thousand a year?" The words scarcely peeped from her throat.

"Mmm-hmm." His eyes lingered indolently on hers as he clamped those perfect teeth around the second mushroom. Mesmerized, still not quite able to absorb his offer, she watched as he ate all four mushrooms.

Forty thousand dollars!

"You must be joking."

"Not at all. You'll work damn hard for it. If I say travel, you'll travel. We're bidding jobs in about eight states right now. Sometimes there'll be late nights if we're up against a deadline. Other times there'll be night flights in order to get connections to the right city. I pay my estimators well, but they earn every cent of it."

She was still too stunned to take it all in. "I don't even know where your offices are."

"On the other side of the creek, near Rainbow and Johnson Drive. I'll take you over later to see them, if you like."

Again she was astonished. The area he'd named was well known as one of the most prestigious in the city. It was generally referred to as the Plaza Area, named after the lush Country Club Plaza Shopping Center nearby. She was still pondering this when Sam Brown pulled a tie from the pocket of his blue linen sport coat, though she was so lost in thought she scarcely realized what he was doing. Without the aid of a mirror, he raised his collar, lay the tie underneath, buttoned his collar button, and began applying a Windsor knot to the tie by feel. Though her eyes were fixed on his hands, she was thinking instead of the pair of widewale corduroy armchairs she wanted so badly, thinking of the drapes she could pay off in no time, thinking of not having to give up the townhouse.

The ever-attentive Walter appeared as if out of nowhere. "Will there be anything more, Mr. Brown?"

"Ms. Walker and I will go into dinner now, Walter. Thank you."

"Of course, sir. I'll bring your drinks for you."

Lee finally slipped out of her reverie to realize that Sam Brown was slipping a hand under her elbow and urging her to her feet. They followed at Walter's heels. "House rules," Sam whispered conspiratorially. "Men have to wear ties in the dining room."

Lee made a feeble attempt to pull away from his commanding grasp. This is all too perfect. It's going too fast!

"I'm not dressed—"

"You're dressed just fine." His eyes swept her from hair to her waist, and up again.

She felt obligated to resist one more time. "But . . . but I haven't even said I'd work for you, much less won a bid yet. And you invited me for a drink, not dinner."

He only grinned down at her cheek, squeezed the soft, bare skin of her inner elbow, and teased, "Let a man try to impress a lady when he's trying his damndest, okay, Cherokee?"

That word, perhaps more than any other, brought her back down to earth. Cherokee. But it was too late now. They'd reached the dining room doorway, which opened off the lounge. She felt helpless as she was propelled along beside him. His thumb was rough on her bare skin as they paused just inside, and he was again greeted by name. "Evening, Mr. Brown . . . ma'am. Your table is all ready." The man escorted them to a linen-covered table in front of a wide window that curved in a semicircle around half of the dining room. Lee looked onto a view of the swimming pool, ice rink, and tennis courts below. In the distance a line of tall trees indicated the meandering route of Brush Creek as it flowed eastward. The sun was slanting across the green lawn, from which Lee had difficulty pulling her eyes.

A nudge on the back of her knees reminded her that Sam Brown was solicitously waiting to push in her chair.

"Oh . . . thank you." She settled herself, subjected to the tantalizing scent that wafted about him as he sat down across from her. He had no more than hit the chair when yet another solicitous employee of the Carriage Club was immediately at hand to state, "The evening special is shrimp marinated in wine sauce, seasoned with tarragon and served with herb butter. And how are you this evening, Mr. Brown?" Menus were opened crisply and placed first in Lee's hands, then Sam's.

He raised his dark brows, and a smile lifted his lips. "Hungry as a bear, Edward, and how are you?"

Edward leaned back and laughed softly. "I'm fine, sir. Leaving on my vacation tomorrow morning for my son's house in Tucson. He's got a new baby, you know, and we've never seen her."

"I imagine it's a little hard to keep your mind on marinated shrimp then, isn't it?"

"For you, sir, not at all. Service is the same as always."

They laughed together in the way of men who go through this ritual often. Lee noted the same camaraderie between Brown and yet another man who brought them goblets of ice water.

When they were alone with their menus at last, Lee admitted, "I am impressed, Brown. How could I help but be?"

"Tell me that when you've seen me in action in the office and it'll mean something."

She looked for signs of teasing and saw none.

This man, this Sam Brown, what did she know of him? Was he honorable or a scoundrel? Was his poise in these elegant surroundings an intentional smoke screen to hide his seamier side? He could charm the gold out of a person's teeth—she had no doubt about that—but could he also be ruthless? He was handsome enough to turn any woman's head, and that fact made it more difficult to assess his hidden traits. After all, she was making a business decision, and what he looked like had absolutely no bearing upon his character or his motives. Studying him now, Lee entwined her fingers, pressed her arms along the table edge, and bent forward until her breasts touched her wrists.

"Level with me, Brown. Would you hire me with the ulterior motive of exploiting me, like Thorpe did?"

She watched his eyes carefully as they registered

faint surprise at her direct question, then glinted with brief amusement before that too disappeared and he asked matter-of-factly, "Could it be, Ms. Walker, that you have a hang-up about being Indian?" Immediately she bristled, but before she could respond he went on. "I did a little checking on you. You're good, you're honest, you're young and ambitious. A man could do worse than hire a person like that as an estimator, especially when his corporation has all its officers intact. Besides that, it wouldn't be far for you to drive. That's always to an employer's advantage."

His answer set her back in her chair. "How do you know where I live?"

Again a glint of amusement filled his eyes. "You forget. Your suitcase had a tag on its handle just like mine did."

Of course! How could she forget what had led her here in the first place? Yet it was disconcerting to think he'd been asking people about her.

"Tell me, Mr. Brown," she began, "is there anything you don't know about me?"

He looked up from his menu and she became uncomfortably aware that she was wearing a necklace shaped like an Indian arrowhead strung around her neck on a leather thong. But his eyes returned to his menu as he answered, "Yes, I don't know why you bother to order your meals without potatoes when you don't need to. The food here is tremendous. Don't stint yourself tonight."

His answer raised an instant prickle of female vanity, but she warned herself to accept the compliment with a grain of salt. Just then the waiter approached to take their order.

The meal was delicious, as promised. They ate it while discussing upcoming jobs Sam would want her to bid, projects she had worked on, nothing more personal until, over coffee, he sat back with one shoulder drooping lower than the other in a way with which she was already becoming familiar.

"Actually, there is a question about you that puzzles me," he said.

She looked up, waiting.

"Why don't you have records of employment before Thorpe Construction?"

"I do. They're in St. Louis."

"St. Louis?" Sam quirked an eyebrow.

"Yes, that's where I lived before."

"Before what?" Though his eyes rested lightly on her, she had the feeling he was drilling into her head.

"Before I moved here three years ago," she answered with deliberate evasion.

"Ah." He tilted his chin up, and for a moment she thought he might question her further, but just then the waiter arrived and laid a small tray at Sam Brown's elbow and handed him a silver pen.

"Excuse me, Mr. Brown, your tab." Sam scrawled a quick signature and rose to his feet.

"Come on, I'll show you the office."

Lee breathed a sigh of relief at the interruption, for the subject of St. Louis was not one she wanted to pursue.

As they moved past the tables toward the doorway, they were interrupted by an impeccably dressed man who leaned back in a chair, half turning to extend a hand. "How's it going, Sam?"

"Fine. Took a job in Denver last week." Brown released his hold on Lee's elbow to shake hands, then politely performed introductions.

"Cassie and Don Norris . . . Lee Walker, my newest estimator."

Lee considered spouting a denial aloud, but instead she politely shook hands with the Norrises.

"Well, congratulations, Lee. You've chosen a damn fine company there," Don Norris offered. She murmured some comment, surprised at his unsolicited praise and hoping it was true. A moment later Sam urged her toward the door again.

As they moved through the lounge, she couldn't resist glancing up at Sam. "Your new estimator? Aren't you being a little presumptuous?"

Sam smiled and shrugged. "It eliminated a lengthy explanation. I could have said you were the woman who stole my suitcase in the Denver airport. Would that have been better?"

Lee turned to hide her grin as they reached the main lobby, crossed to the door, and stepped outside.

"You can ride with me," he suggested. "It's not far, and I can bring you back to your car afterward."

He led her to a classy, off-white Toronado. Inside, the car smelled like him—the agreeably masculine and tangy scent of what she took to be Rawhide cosmetics. The front seat was luxurious, equipped with a stereo that filled the void while they drove in the waning summer evening.

It had been a long time since Lee had been in a car with an attractive man—and Sam Brown was certainly that! She watched the contour of his wrist draped over the steering wheel, the gleam of a gold watch peeking from beneath his sleeve, the relaxed fingers with dark skin and well-kept nails. She recalled the pleasant meal they'd just shared, his easygoing camaraderie with everyone at the club, the compliment Norris had dropped in passing, Brown's glib sense of humor. She ventured a brief study of his hair, an ear, the side of his neck, but then his face swung her way and she looked quickly out her side window.

No doubt about it—she was beginning to like Sam Brown.

The office complex was new, modern, and pleasing to the eye. The late sun, slanting across its cinnamon-colored brick walls and smoked-glass windows, created deep triangles of shadow, accentuating the beauty of the buildings' architectural design. In keeping with Kansas City's claim that it had more fountains than any other city in the world except Rome, the buildings had been designed around a charming esplanade whose main attraction was a fountain whose running water created a design reminiscent of a dandelion gone to seed.

Sam guided Lee along curved concrete walks past cherry trees, and yews and more, every shrub so well-kept it appeared they were tended by a beautician instead of a gardener. The sprinkler system had come on, and as they sauntered between the buildings Lee breathed in the pungent scent of wet cedar chips clustered at the base of the decorative plants. Redwood benches had been placed strategically along the walks, and even the trash depositories were built of redwood, blending pleasantly into the environment. Tall ash trees had been planted alongside each building.

Sam unlocked the lobby door and held it open while Lee entered a spacious foyer carpeted in burnt orange. The stairs were carpeted as well and seemed to drop out of nowhere into the center of the lobby. A rich walnut handrail was smooth beneath Lee's palm as she ran her hand along it appreciatively.

If she'd expected Brown to be a smalltime hood, his surroundings were suggesting otherwise.

At Suite 204 he fitted a key into the lock, pushed the walnut door inward, and held it also as she passed before him. Fluorescent lights came on, flooding the reception area.

Lee glanced around nervously. There was something so gloomy and deserted about the silent, empty office. The room was decorated in tones of blue, from royal to wedgwood, and the walls were hung with posters depicting various moments in the company's history. They were framed in aluminum, fronted with glass, and hung on rich vinyl wallcovering that matched upholstered chairs and smoked-glass tables, where various construction magazines and equipment brochures lay.

The chink of keys brought Lee's attention back to Sam.

"This is obviously the reception area," he said, motioning her ahead of him around a free-standing wall that formed the backdrop for the receptionist's desk.

The payroll office was the first cubicle behind the wall. Inside, a computer hummed softly and photographs of two toddlers stood on a desk.

"The computer runs day and night," Sam informed Lee. "All our payroll and parts inventory are stored in it."

There was a separate office for the bookkeeper and his assistant, followed by a large open area, also carpeted in deep blue, where slant-topped drafting tables were lined up. The arrangement preserved an overall feeling of space, for the smoky windows ran nearly ceiling to floor, and the sight of the ash trees outside helped bring the outdoors in. The suite was at the southeast corner of the building, thus the fading sun left this area dimly lit, for Sam hadn't turned on the overhead lights here.

"This is where our draftsmen work," he explained unnecessarily. Lee was ever conscious of him hovering a step behind her. Occasionally the soft clink of keys told her how near he was. She looked across the pleasant, orderly expanse. Wide racks of blueprints hung neatly, like sheets on a clothesline. There were no rolled, wrinkled, or torn plans in sight. There were no chunks of dried clay on the carpet, no coffee-can cuspidors. "That's the copy room." Sam pointed, and Lee turned her head in time to catch the vague movement of his arm before he moved through the drafting area into a separate corner office. In the doorway he turned again to her, his stance inviting her in.

"Yours?" she asked.

He nodded.

Just inside the door she stopped, tingles of appreciation running along her arms. The room was neat and orderly, and Lee couldn't help comparing it to

Floyd Thorpe's pigpen. A modest-sized executive desk stood to one side, a credenza under the window. There was a game table, surrounded by rich leather armchairs on ball castors, which was obviously used as a conference table. The floor was carpeted in rich chocolate, the windows treated with vertical blinds of a lighter shade. Here again, plans and blueprints hung on neat racks. A tall schefflera plant stood in the corner where east and south-facing windows met.

Lee crossed to the south window and looked out. A moment later her nostrils were again filled with Sam's scent as he stepped behind her and pointed past the treetops. "That's where we were." From here she could see only the tip of the Carriage Club's main building. "Most of the time I move in a rather confined area."

"But a very pleasant one," she noted, turning and laying her fingertips on the polished surface of his desk. Her eyes met his, but there was no hint of teasing in them this time. "I like it very much."

The expression on his face told Lee it was one thing he'd wanted to hear. His fingers relaxed and the keys clinked softly.

"Would you like to see the estimating area?"

"I thought you'd never ask."

A smile broke on his face like sun over the horizon, and he led the way to another wide expanse much like that where the drafting tables were. Here the tables were flat and of desk height. The southern exposure gave the estimating area the same view as that from Sam's office. Lee looked out, thinking again of the three years she'd worked in Floyd Thorpe's office, wondering if she could possibly be wrong about Sam Brown's character, knowing it was fast losing importance in light of his fantastic offer and this enticing office.

"You're the first full-time estimator I've hired for the new portion of the business, so there's no designated area for you," Sam explained. "You'll just work in here with the plumbing estimators, if that's all right with you."

"Oh . . ." She turned from the window. "That's more than all right, as I'm sure you're well aware. I've never seen a contractor's office as plush as this. But I'm sure you're well aware of that, too."

"Just because you dig in dirt for a living doesn't mean you have to live in it."

"No, not at all. Somebody should tell that to Floyd Thorpe."

He turned and indicated a desk across the way. "That would be yours."

The desks were placed in herringbone relationship to one another, giving the room an even more spacious aspect. Beside the desk Sam was pointing to stood a potted orange tree that seemed to be thriving.

Lee crossed to *her* desk, pulled out *her* chair, and touched *her* orange tree. The chair rolled silently on a large slab of clear vinyl that protected the blue carpet. She sat down, and placed her palms flat on the desk top as if to test its temperature. A feeling of imminent excitement tightened her chest. My God, it was like a dream come true. She looked up at Sam, standing some distance across the room, watching every move she made.

"I think it fits." Accepting his offer, she was filled with anticipation.

"Agreed." He raised a hand and beckoned her over to him. "Come on, I'll drive you back to your car. You'll be spending enough time in that chair without staying in it now."

She pushed the chair back beneath the desk and moved to him. This time he didn't touch her, but before they rounded the corner she turned back, taking one last look at her desk.

BACK in his car she didn't hear the music, didn't feel the plush seat, didn't watch his wrist on the wheel. She was too excited.

"My God, Brown, did you do all that or did your father?"

"He made it possible for me to do it. We didn't have that office until after he died."

She paused. "I imagine he would have loved it as much as I do."

"He was content at the old location," Sam said. "My mother was the one who encouraged me to move into the new building and add a touch of class to the operation. It turned out we'd made too damn much profit one year. The overhead became a healthy tax write-off after we rented this new place. Meanwhile we enjoy the surroundings."

"You know what I want to do the first day of work?" Lee rested her head back against the luxurious seat and closed her eyes.

"What?"

She rolled her head toward Sam and opened her eyes to find him studying the curve of her arched throat. "I want to bring my sack lunch and sit by that fountain and eat at high noon."

He laughed pleasantly, and she watched his lips change with the sound. "Whatever turns you on. There are several good restaurants in the complex—"

"Restaurants! Where's your sense of . . . of nature!"

"I get all the nature I need during the day. I spend more than half my time at jobsites. My old man taught me that's the only way to run a business—by keeping your eye on what's happening instead of leaving it up to someone else. At noon I like to go where it's cool and not dusty and let somebody serve me a decent meal on a plate."

Lee couldn't help wondering if he went out on the job dressed like that. His brown shoes certainly didn't look like they'd scuffed any dust today.

Just then, the Toronado turned into the horseshoe driveway of the Carriage Club, and Lee straightened in her seat. Brown swung the car into a parking spot, and before she could protest he was out his side and heading around to open her door. She beat him to the punch and met him beside the car.

He turned and together they ambled across the lot. "When do you want to start?" he asked.

She stopped him with a hand on his sleeve. "Brown, there's just one thing I have to ask for even before I say I'll take the job."

"What's that?"

She swallowed, knowing that what she had to ask was presumptuous. "I . . . I have to have the last week of August off." This was the last week of July—she knew it was a lot to ask. Nobody in the construction industry took time off during the busy summer season. As she stood waiting for Sam's response, she feared, too, that he might demand the reason for her request and sought frantically for a white lie. But in the end she had no need to produce one.

"Shouldn't be any problem," Sam said, "but usually

we take vacations during the cold months when there's not much going on." He began moving on, but Lee grabbed his arm.

"Oh, I didn't mean I expect it off with pay! It's just . . ." She grew self-conscious holding his arm and dropped her hand.

"It's okay. As far as I can remember, there won't be any important bids around that time, so you can plan on it as yours."

"Thank you. In that case, back to your original question." She braved a sheepish smile. "Would Monday be too soon to start?"

He chuckled, came back to where she trailed along behind him, and lightly pressed a palm against the small of her back. "Are you that eager to work for this . . . reprobate?" he teased.

Moving toward her car, she admitted artlessly, "I need to make the house payment next week, just like you do." She was far too aware of the warmth of his palm through the thin knit of her top, but then it disappeared.

"I don't make house payments. I live in the old family rattrap with my mother."

This was the second time he'd mentioned his mother, and Lee couldn't help but wonder. Another case of apron strings? Though she'd never have thought it of Sam Brown, she'd learned her lesson once with Joel. Furthermore, Sam wasn't the only one who'd done some calculating after reading an address on a suitcase. The family "rattrap" of which he spoke was on exclusive Ward Parkway. She didn't have to see the house to imagine what it must be like.

"Speaking of rattraps"—they'd reached her Pinto—"this one is mine."

He gave it a cursory glance, then returned his attention to her. "Is there anything else you need to know about the job?"

"Nothing I can think of. Oh, what are office hours?"

"On a normal day I usually come in around seven and knock off at five."

There seemed little more to say, and while she studied Sam Brown's expression, it ceased to say "business" and took on the distinctly alarming look of "pleasure."

A slow hand reached for the silver arrowhead necklace that rested against her chest, still warm from her skin, and his eyes followed. His fingers closed around it, and she thought she felt the thong tighten at the back of her neck.

Panic clawed its way up to her throat. She wanted to say "Brown, don't!" for she thought he was going to kiss her and, since he was about to become her boss, she couldn't let him set such a dangerous precedent. She wanted his job, but no other complications. Besides, he lived on Ward Parkway in the family "rattrap" with his mother . . . and . . . and . . . oh God, Brown, you smell so good . . . let go . . .

But she was never to know Sam Brown's intentions, for a moment later he dropped the arrowhead against her chest and turned away before an enormous sneeze erupted from him.

Lee was laughing before the second sneeze clutched him. He tugged a hanky from his hip pocket, rubbed his nose, and stepped back three feet.

"You and your damn Renaldo la Pizzio!"

Even though she jammed her hands on her hips, Lee was still amused as she scolded, "Oh, you had yourself a regular heyday with my private belongings, didn't you?"

"I could order you to get rid of it before you show up at the office."

"You could, but you won't. After all, they write exposés in Washington about orders like that."

But even as she chuckled, her body felt weak with relief, for if he *had* tried to kiss her, she wasn't sure how long she'd have resisted.

Chapter

FIVE

T HE night before her first day of work, Lee slept in that tenuous half-conscious state she often experienced before a day promising something special—a thin, filmy kind of sleep during which the excitement somehow managed to keep her so nearly alert that the morning alarm was stifled before its bell gave out more than a ting. She lay staring at the ceiling, which was tinted pale pink by the rising sun, and said in amazement, "Forty thousand dollars a year, can you beat that?"

Then she was on her feet, eagerness in every step as she switched on the radio, showered, washed her hair, took a sinful amount of time styling it, then applied her makeup. Her head was tilted back, a mascara wand darkening her stubby lashes, when she suddenly straightened, stared at her reflection, smiled, and told the woman in the mirror, "An orange tree . . . You have an orange tree by your desk!" Then the woman in the mirror replied, "Damn fool, Walker, finish your primping or you'll be late on your first day."

Lee considered long and hard before deciding between a warm rose slack outfit and a white slim skirt with a matching peplumed jacket. She chose the skirt in deference to the classy office, the white in deference to her own deep coloring. It complemented her dark skin and black hair so strikingly that Lee felt thoroughly pleased with her appearance when she was all dressed. The straight skirt added to her height and the peplum added to her hips—an altogether flattering combo. After adding a single white bangle bracelet that matched white hoops in her ears, she was satisfied.

But as she smoothed the skirt one last time over her hips, she confronted her reflection in the mirror again and a worried frown formed between her eyebrows. Had she dressed so carefully to please Sam Brown? The possibility was disturbing. She dropped her eyes to the photographs of Jed and Matthew in a hinged frame on her dresser top. The familiar stab of loss cut through her momentarily, then she was removing the black combs that held her hair behind each ear, replacing them defiantly with others that trailed small, bronze feathers to the backs of her jaws.

You are what you are, Lee Walker, and you'd be wise not to forget it!

In the office Sam Brown seemed to scarcely notice what she was wearing. The sleeves of his plaid shirt were already rolled up past the elbows, and he held a set of plans in his hand. Though he greeted Lee with a pleasant, "Good morning . . . all set to meet the gang?" it was all business with Sam Brown.

Three others were already there when Lee arrived. Sam immediately introduced her as "the first permanent employee of the sewer and water division." Rachael Robinson, the office's gal friday, was efficient and energetic. She wore a pale yellow dress that looked smashing against her black skin and conveyed a very *now* look.

Immediately Lee could tell Frank Schultz was Sam Brown's right-hand man. Schultz was the head estimator of plumbing and had been working with Sam on the few sewer and water jobs they'd bid so far. A bull-headed Irishman named Duke was head superintendent of the outside crews, and under him worked several foremen who remained voices on the radio much of the time. Ron Chen was head bookkeeper, a small Chinese man with thick glasses and an ingratiating smile. His second in command was his own twenty-year-old daughter, Terri, who worked part time and attended the University of Missouri at Kansas City the rest of the week. The computer was manned by an older, portly woman named Nelda Huffman, who looked more like a cleaning lady than a payroll clerk. The pictures on Nelda's desk proved to be of her grandchildren.

By the time all the employees of Brown & Brown had begun their work day, Lee Walker felt as if she were in the amphitheater of the United Nations Building! She realized that nobody here would notice a feather in her hair, although Rachael did comment on how stylish it was.

Brown & Brown was a pleasant change from Thorpe Construction. Though Lee didn't have her own office as she'd had previously, she didn't mind a bit. Among the entire office crew there was a noticeable camaraderie that made up for the lack of privacy. And the atmosphere was so harmonious, the decor so tasteful, that Lee felt almost childishly eager to do well, learn fast, and prove her abilities so she could feel justified in taking over the desk and the orange tree.

At coffee break the copy room became a gathering spot. It contained not only copying and duplicator machines, but also a refrigerator, microwave oven, and coffee percolator that was kept constantly replenished by Rachael, who seemed to be the office staff's cheerful "ladybug." Everyone seemed to like her.

The day began with a short session at which Sam Brown, Frank Schultz, and Rachael discussed helping Lee learn her way around the place. After Lee had filled out the usual new-employee forms, Frank explained the general bidding procedure, psychology, and ratio of profit on which they worked.

Sam was gone at noon, and Lee ate her sack lunch by the fountain, feeling totally refreshed when she returned. She saw Sam again late in the afternoon when he came in briefly, dusty leather workboots and khaki-colored jeans attesting to his having been out in the field. When Frank Schultz began cleaning off his desk top at the end of the afternoon, Lee couldn't believe it was going on five o'clock already. The day had raced by so fast it seemed as if she'd just walked in the door!

The following morning she, Sam, and Frank worked together on a small bid. Immediately Lee saw that changes here were discussed sensibly before being made. No last minute surprises were sprung unless it was by mutual agreement. They talked together about upcoming jobs listed in *The Construction Bulletin* and decided which ones Lee should order plans for. Sam asked if Frank would have time the following day to take Lee out and show her around the jobs in progress so she could get a handle on the equipment the company owned, and also give her a complete inventory of it so she knew exactly what work capacity they could handle.

The third day, she and Frank drove in a company pickup, from jobsite to jobsite. At each, Lee was introduced to crew members and foremen alike.

Walking into the skeleton of a two-story steel-frame building, Lee was surprised to see Sam Brown, in hardhat and workboots, waving hello. He picked his way across pipes and fittings, removing a pair of soiled leather workgloves as he came.

"Got troubles, boss?" Frank inquired.

"Naw, nothing Duke can't handle." Sam smiled over his shoulder as Lee heard Duke in the background, his voice like the roar of a bull elephant, telling some laborer to jack that son of a bitch up and see she didn't bust again or his ass'd be higher than the goddam water table! Lee was laughing as Sam turned back to her. The rough language of construction superintendents was nothing new to her.

"Everything going okay so far, Lee?" Sam's question was simple and inconsequential, nothing at all to make her heart jump. Maybe it was the ordinary way he'd called her Lee, or the way he lifted his hardhat off the back of his head and mopped his forehead with a sleeve that sent her pulse racing.

"Not a single complaint," she answered. "We've been to all the jobsites but one. I'm getting a good idea of how much equipment the company has, but I can see there's not much in the way of heavy stuff."

"We've leased most of the heavy stuff up till now and we'll continue to do that until we're sure we want to stay in the sewer and water work," Sam explained.

"A couple of the jobs we discussed yesterday would require a nine-eighty front-end loader and I haven't seen one yet."

"I know. We don't own one. The biggest we've got is a nine-fifty. That's why I wanted you to make the rounds with Frank. I've got some decisions to make about buying new equipment, and I want you in on them." There was something elemental about him standing in the hot sun with a dusty boot on a section of pipe, settling the hardhat back on his head, then tugging back on the filthy leather gloves. His rolled-up sleeves exposed arms tanned to a cinnamon hue with hair bleached almost red by the sun. A bead of sweat trickled from under the hardhat along his temple, and Lee looked away.

In the background a machine started up, and Sam shouted to be heard above the noise. "Frank, could you run out to the Independence City Hall and pick up a set of plans for that Little Blue River job?"

"Sure, Sam. We'll be over that direction anyway."

"Good. Lee and I will run out and take a look at it Friday morning." At the mention of her name, she turned back to the trickle of sweat, but it had become no less irresistible, collecting dust as it moved downward. It drew her eyes as if it were whitewater on the Colorado River rather than a single droplet flowing along a man's hairline.

She pulled her eyes away again, hoping Sam hadn't noticed the direction of her gaze. At first she thought he hadn't, but in the end she wasn't sure, for as Frank pulled the pickup away from the bumpy construction site, Lee looked back over her shoulder to discover Sam standing where they'd left him, his feet planted firmly apart, his eyes following them.

O N Thursday, just before Lee left for the day, Sam stopped by her desk. "It's been a helluva busy week. Sorry I haven't been around much."

Lee's elbows were propped on the desk top as she leaned over a long jobsheet. Turning, she almost bumped against Sam's thigh, he'd been standing so close. She tipped her chair back to look up at him.

"Frank has taken good care of me. The week's been great."

Sam crossed his arms, leaned against the edge of her desk, and stretched his legs out in front of him. "Good, glad to hear it. Listen, would you mind wearing something . . ." For a moment his eyes fell to her bare knee where her skirt was hitched up slightly.

"Well, put on some slacks tomorrow, okay? We'll probably be walking through some rough stuff when we go out to look at that job."

"Sure, whatever you say."

"Have you got any boots?" Now his eyes drifted down her calves to the sling-back high heels on her feet.

"Aha. Got just the thing."

"Good. Bring 'em along. We'll be going out first thing in the morning, and the dew can be heavy."

"Anything else?"

"Yeah." For the first time he glanced up to give a quick survey of the room, but several desks were already empty, and nobody who remained paid them any attention. His gaze returned to Lee. "Have you been bringing those sack lunches like you said?"

"Every day. The fountain is delightful with cheese on rye."

"Could you make enough for two tomorrow?" His eyes softened as he smiled down at her.

"Of course. What's the occasion?"

"No occasion. We might end up someplace out in the boonies at lunchtime, so if you'll bring the food, I'll bring us some cola in a cooler."

"Friday is bologna and pickle day."

"Sweet or dill?"

"Dill."

"Sold." He stood up. "See you here at eight."

* * *

THE following morning dawned murky and muggy after a night of intermittent thundershowers. Low, gray clouds hid the sunrise, and the thick, sultry air seemed cloyingly sticky.

She dressed in blue jeans, tennis shoes, and a casual cotton knit pullover of navy and white stripes with a sailor collar and a ribbed waist, and took along a pair of rubber, lace-up duck hunting boots, a can of mosquito spray, and a brown paper bag containing three bologna sandwiches, potato chips, pickles, and some chocolate chip cookies.

She and Sam set out right after he returned from his morning rounds of all the jobs. He stopped at Rachael's desk to advise her where they'd be. "If you need us, give a call on the radio."

"Right, boss."

"We'll take my truck," Sam informed Lee as they crossed the parking lot toward a sleek pickup identifiable by its standard company color—a rich, metallic brown with the logo B & B in white on its doors. Sam looked down at Lee's feet.

"Didn't you bring any boots?"

"They're in my car. Be right back." She was only too happy to move away from Sam Brown, for her eyes, too, had meandered down the length of his strong legs, and the sight of them was altogether too compelling. What was it about him? Whenever she was close to him her thoughts strayed to his masculinity, ever since that first night in Denver when she'd found his magazine.

He'd backed the pickup around and was waiting when she turned from the Pinto with full hands. This time her eyes were arrested by the sight of his long, bronzed arm in its white rolled-up sleeve as he stretched across the truck seat to push the door open for her. *Shape up, Lee Walker, and think business!* Dragging her thoughts back to safer footing, she clambered up onto the high seat beside him and dumped her collection on the floor.

A roll of plans, his workgloves and hardhat lay between them, and with a murmured apology, Sam scooped them closer to his hip to make more room for her.

"It's okay," Lee assured him, flashing him a quick smile.

But it wasn't okay. There was something too close about the relatively confining space of the single seat. And—dammit!—did Sam Brown's vehicles always have to smell like him? It was his world, this masculine domain of hardhats, laced-up leather boots, and pickups with column shifts.

"I'll drive, you navigate," Sam ordered as they started out. Almost gratefully, Lee opened the wide set of plans and studied the map. But even so, she found herself too aware of the tan arm with its relaxed wrist that shifted gears, the hand vibrating on the stick. Covertly she watched the tightening of muscles beneath the left leg of his blue jeans as he raised it to press in the clutch. He was a runner, she remembered, and supposed those muscles were hard and well toned. The denim fit his leg like a rind fits an orange.

Suddenly she realized they were sitting still and raised her eyes from Sam's leg to find he'd been watching her. For how long? She felt herself turning as red as the light that had stopped them as he smiled lazily.

"I see you brought the bologna sandwiches." His face was stunningly dark against the open collar of his white shirt, and it did foolish things to the pit of her stomach.

"As ordered. Where's the Coke?" she managed to ask in a surprisingly normal voice.

He gestured with a shoulder and a lift of his chin. "In the back." His lazy eyes made her feel light-headed, but just then the light changed and they rolled forward. Sam's gaze moved away from her, and she returned to navigating.

"Exit on Two ninety-one south," she ordered.

"Two ninety-one south," he repeated. Then there was only the high whine of the wheels on the blacktop and the shuddering jiggle rising up through the seat beneath Lee as they rode silently. She watched the riffling of his shirtsleeves in the wind from the opened window, then studied the view beyond her own, striving to feel at ease in his presence.

Suddenly Rachael's voice crackled across the radio. "Base to unit one. Come in, Sam."

From the corner of her eye, Lee watched him pluck the mike from the dash. His index finger curled around the call button and the mike almost touched his lips. "Unit one, Sam here. Go ahead, Rachael."

"I've got a long-distance call from Denver. It's Tom Weatherall returning your call, so I thought you'd want to know."

"It's nothing important, just an inquiry I made about an equipment auction that's coming up. Tell him I'll get back to him on Monday."

"Right, boss . . . base clear."

"Thanks, Rachael. Unit one clear."

The white shirtsleeve strained diagonally across Sam's upper arm as he replaced the mike, and Lee turned her eyes resolutely away, again resisting the urge to study him. But to her chagrin, she found she need not look to remember. He was dressed in blue jeans, white shirt, and leather boots—no different from what a thousand laboring men wore every day. Yet he looked better than a thousand men, the basic no-nonsense work clothes lending him a magnetic sex appeal totally different from the dress slacks and sport coat he'd worn the first few times she'd seen him.

Keep your mind on your map, Walker, he didn't even kiss you.

They turned off 291 at her directions and took increasingly smaller roads until they came to a gravel road that led out into the country. "I think this is it." Lee pointed to an abandoned farm off to their right.

The pickup swerved to the side of the road to idle again while Sam hooked his left elbow over the steering wheel, rested his right hand along the back of the seat, and peered out her window. She was served up a tantalizing whiff of his aftershave as his knuckles passed before her face and he pointed.

"Looks like it'll start just this side of those trees and move off across the edge of that field. We might as well get out and walk it."

Lee was only too glad to escape the close proximity to Sam Brown, and she jumped from the cab with a shaky, indrawn breath of relief. She sat down on the running board to untie her tennis shoes and replace them with the olive drab waterproof boots, conscious now that Sam was standing with his hands on his hips watching her. She tucked her pantlegs into the boot tops, but left the yellow strings dangling. Still he stood, his weight balanced evenly on both feet, making her skin prickle with awareness. It had been a long time since a man had watched her change her clothes, even any as impersonal as shoes, and this man seemed to be studying the process all too closely. She straightened, got to her feet, and gave her ribbed waistband a businesslike tug to pull it back into place. His face wore a disturbingly appreciative half grin, his gaze centered on the thin band of skin at her waist, which quickly disappeared as she adjusted her shirt.

"What are you staring at, Brown?" she demanded.

He seemed to shake himself back to the present. "Estimators look different than they used to," he teased.

Keep it light, her saner self warned as his comment aroused a small thrill. She displayed one foot, lifting it before her. "Same as you, jeans and boots."

But as his eyes traveled down to her boots, she realized that instead of minimizing her femininity, they accented it. To her relief, at that moment Sam's hand slapped at his neck, then he made a grab at the air, missing the mosquito that had just bitten him.

"Come here, I'll give you a spray." Lee picked up the can from the floor of the truck.

With a grin, he noted, "You come prepared, don't you?"

"In Missouri, in August, the morning after a healthy rain?" she asked pointedly. He came to stand before her while she shook the can and sprayed the front of him in long sweeps from neck to boots, noting even in that quick journey certain spots where his jeans were more worn. *Damn you, Walker, what's the matter with you?* "Turn around, I'll do your back." But his back presented as enticing a set of muscles as his front. His shoulders were wide and firm as she sprayed them, heading down toward where his shirt scarcely crinkled as it disappeared into the narrow waist of his jeans. His buns were so flat that they scarcely curved beneath the denim. Again she remembered that he was a runner. It seemed a long, long way down to his wide-spread boots.

He craned to look at her over his shoulder. "Hurry up. This stuff stinks."

As she stood up, she couldn't resist teasing. "Don't be such a baby, Brown. I don't think it smells so bad." And as if to prove the point, she gave him a shot inside the back of his collar, then pulled the can farther back and emitted a cloud at the back of his head. He doubled forward and let out an immense sneeze.

She burst out laughing as he moved out of range and whirled.

"Damn it all, if it isn't one thing it's another."

She puckered her face and feigned an apology. "Oh, I'm so-o-o sorry."

A wicked grin lifted his mouth as he returned wryly, "Yes, I can see just how sorry you are."

He took a menacing step toward her, and she

backed away. "Now, Brown, it was an accident!" she warned, holding out a hand to fend him off. But he advanced a step farther.

"So will this be." He wrenched the can from her hand and shook it, a gleam of menace in his eye.

"Brown, I'm warning you!"

"You started it, now stand and take your medicine."

There was nothing she could do but turn her back on him, squeeze her eyes shut, and wait. He took his sweet time about it, while she grew increasingly uncomfortable. Finally she felt the spray at the back of her neck. Then it moved downward and stopped at her hips. "Put your arms up," he ordered. She gritted her teeth, did as ordered, but immediately realized her mistake, for when her arms went up, so did the shirt. A long moment passed in silence, and she felt herself beginning to blush. Then the hiss of the spray finished its trip down her backside, and he nudged her with the can, ordering, "Turn around." She spun about, chancing a quick peek at the top of his hair as he hunkered down before her, but quickly shutting her eyes as the cloud of spray moved upward. It stopped again, at her hips, and she suffered an agonizing moment, wondering what he was doing before a direct shot hit her in her bare navel.

She yelped and jumped backward. "Damn you, Brown!"

He chuckled devilishly. "I couldn't resist."

She glared at him as he knelt on one knee, his eyes nearly on a level with the ribbed waistband that she now hugged protectively in place. She was fighting a losing battle of trying to forget that Sam Brown was a man—and he wasn't helping one bit! The only resource she could draw upon was feigned indignation. She yanked the can from his hand, then stalked to the truck and flung it through the open window.

"We've got work to do, Brown. Enough of this fooling around!" And, thankfully, he followed her lead and got back down to business.

They set off through knee-high grass laden with dew and embroidered with spider webs to which droplets of moisture clung. They moved slowly, the only sounds those of their footsteps swishing through the grass, which occasionally squeaked as it brushed wetly against Lee's rubber boots. They stopped and stood shoulder to shoulder, each holding one side of the wide blueprints as they studied them.

There were a hundred considerations to be made when deciding whether or not to bid a job such as this one. The first and most obvious was the amount of dirt to be moved, where to, and with what. As they walked, they scanned the ups and downs, considering, discussing, doing mental calculations. They left the fairly level edge of the cornfield and came to a section of uneven roughland—pasture for the most part—with gullies and swales, many filled with muddy potholes after last night's rains. The dampness of the soil was a second important consideration, so Sam and Lee often knelt, side by side, lifting handfuls of soil, noting where they wanted to do test borings.

Lee was conscious of the smell of mosquito spray and wet earth, and of Sam Brown's inviting masculine scent, as they squatted with their shoulders almost touching. They moved on again, following the route the pipe would take, crossing a thick stand of prairie thistle in full purple bloom, until they came to a marsh where red-winged blackbirds perched atop bobbing cattails. The birds' voices raised a cacophony while Sam and Lee stood unmoving for several minutes—just listening and enjoying. It was peaceful and private. Lee became aware that Sam's eyes were seeking her out as he stood behind her, his thumbs hooked on his hipbones. It took great effort to keep from looking back, but she resolutely refrained. Assuming a businesslike air, she noted, "Lots of birds out here."

Sam gave a cursory glance at the swamp and grunted in agreement, but immediately his eyes swung back to her.

"The Department of Natural Resources will require a permit before we mess around with their nesting area. I'll make a note of it." But when she jotted down the note, she braved a glance at him and caught him studying her in a disturbing way. Immediately she looked at the set of plans, but his next question made her forget the figures before her eyes.

"How long have you been divorced?"

The air was utterly still, everything washed clean by the night rains which still lingered on leaf and stem, turning into diamond beads when the sun occasionally broke through the patchy clouds overhead. Lee met Sam's eyes, realizing that if she answered it would be harder than ever to get back to business.

"Three years," she replied.

He seemed to consider before finally asking, "Does he live here?"

"No."

"In St. Louis?"

Though posed in a casual tone, his question brought her to her senses. "We're supposed to be looking for a corner lathe with a red flag on it," she reminded him.

"Oh." He shrugged, as if her deliberate evasion were of little importance. "Oh yeah . . . well, forget I asked."

She tried to do just that, but for the remainder of their walk the unanswered question hung between them.

Chapter
SIX

B Y the time they finished their survey the sun
was high and hot. They had made nearly a
complete circle, which brought them at last to
the foot of a hill below what had once been a thriving
orchard and busy farmhouse. Lee could see the peak
of the roof above the apple trees, and a large, rustic
barn loomed up at her right. As they walked beneath
the laden trees toward the crest of the hill, the shade
felt soothing after the heat of the sun. The orchard
had a scent of its own, a fecund mixture of loam and
ripening fruit. Lee felt the lingering loneliness of
old places whose thriving days have passed.

The house came into view. Like the barn, it had
a fieldstone foundation. To Lee it seemed at once

beautiful and sad, for the dreams that might have nurtured the building of this place were long dead with their dreamers. The voices of its past were long gone. Its windows, vacant now, had once reflected a yard filled with seasonal activity—cattle coming home at the end of deep afternoon, children at play . . .

At the thought, a sharp pain of regret knifed through Lee, and she clutched her stomach.

"Is something wrong?"

"No . . . no!" She turned back to Sam with assumed brightness and made a pretense of rubbing her stomach. "I . . . I'm just hungry, that's all."

He glanced in the direction of the truck. "I can probably make it up that old driveway yet. Why don't you wait here while I get the truck?"

He strode off, and she watched until he disappeared, swallowed up by the trees. The abandoned house drew her irresistibly, and her feet moved almost against her will. She wandered around the foundation, peeking in windows at old linoleum, remnants of wallpaper, a sagging pantry door, a rusted iron pump, a hole in the wall where a chimney had once been. She kicked at a fruit jar that had been left lying in the deep weeds and fought an intense ache brought on by the old place, whose memorabilia brought back memories of her own past.

A gay profusion of tiger lilies nodded on long stems beside the back stoop, and Lee sat down in the sun, dropping her forehead on her crossed arms and raised knees. The truck started, way off in the distance, but she scarcely heard it. Memories came flooding back, memories she wanted to blot out but couldn't— wallpaper on other walls . . . another kitchen sink with a child's dirty feet being washed at bedtime . . . a table with two people, then two plus a baby in a high chair . . . the view from another kitchen window . . . a swing set where a child fell and called for Mommy . . . another back door with a mother swooping through on her way to soothe the child's cries . . . another backyard with day lilies blossoming in lemon brightness . . .

The truck came gunning up the steep, rutted incline, sending rocks rolling behind it, then coming to a stop under the apple trees.

"Lee?" Sam called as he stepped out of the cab. She raised her head slowly, pulling herself back to the present. "Come on down here. It's cooler in the shade." When she didn't move, his hand slipped from the door and his shoulders tensed. "Hey, are you okay?"

He started toward her, and immediately she pulled herself together and jumped off the step, brushing off her backside with a jauntiness she didn't feel.

"Yeah . . . yeah, sure." She would have strode right past him, but he reached out a hand, and before she could prevent it, he swung her around and tipped up her unsteady chin. He studied her closely and, after a long, uncomfortable scrutiny, stated, "You've been crying."

She squelched the sudden, overwhelming urge to throw herself into his arms.

"I have not," she declared stubbornly.

He dropped his eyes to her nostrils, and she made an effort to keep them from quivering. His gaze continued down to her lips, which felt puffy, then back up to her glistening eyes and damp lashes.

"Do you want to talk about it?" he invited very quietly.

No . . . yes . . . oh, please, let me go before I do . . . His eyes invited her confidence, and the corners of his lips turned down as she hovered on the brink of telling him everything, which would prove utterly disastrous, she was sure.

"No," she finally answered.

He seemed to consider for a moment, then his hand fell, and his voice came gay and bright. "All right. Then we'll just eat our lunch." He swung blithely toward the cab, reached inside, and came up with the sack lunch, then left the truck door open and the radio tuned to a country station as he turned to assess the area under the apple trees. "The ground's probably wet. Why don't we sit on the tailgate?"

"Fine," Lee answered, still thrown off guard by Sam's sudden levity when she had expected him to press her for answers. He lowered the tailgate, set the bag down, and turned to her with the same carefree air.

"Need a boost?" Before she could answer, Lee found herself deposited on the cool, brown metal. The truck bounced a little as Sam joined her then twisted to retrieve the cooler and pull out two icy cans of cola before popping their tops and handing her one. He tipped up his own and swilled nearly half its contents before licking his lips, running a hand across his mouth, and sighing with satisfaction.

He looked down pointedly at the sandwich bag between their hips, and Lee realized she'd been watching him with undivided interest, trying to figure him out.

"Oh! Help yourself," she offered.

"Thanks."

He took a sandwich, sank his teeth into it, and swung his feet in rhythm to the soft country songs coming from the cab behind them.

"Aren't you going to eat?" he asked.

Lee was brought back from her wool-gathering and, dutifully taking a bite of the sandwich, discovered she was hungrier than she'd thought. Soon they were sitting in companionable silence, munching and sipping, listening to the birds and the radio.

When Sam finished eating, he leaned back on one palm, hooked a boot heel over the edge of the tailgate, and draped his elbow indolently over an updrawn knee, swinging the cola can idly between his fingers. Lee grew increasingly aware of his scrutiny and of the privacy of the old orchard and abandoned farmyard.

"Are you still hung up on your husband?" Startled, Lee turned to find Sam's brown eyes steady on her face. They were undeniably stunning, their lashes longer than her own. His unsmiling lips had a symmetry and fullness that must have broken a heart or two in their time, she thought.

Unsettled by her observation, she looked at some distant point and answered, "No."

"That's not why you were crying, then?"

She gave up the senseless argument that she hadn't been crying. "I . . . no."

"Over somebody else, then?"

"No, there's nobody else."

A long silence followed, and she sensed him looking at her hair, then at her profile. "Well, then . . ." The ensuing pause was electric. She still felt his eyes on her face but was afraid to look at him. The hand with the can left his knee, then a single, cold index finger lifted her chin until she was forced to meet his eyes. She stared mutely into them—stunning, steady brown eyes—telling herself to turn away sensibly. Instead, she sat as if transfixed as his lips moved closer . . . and closer . . .

"Brown, don't," she said at the last moment, turning aside. Her voice was reedy and strained.

"Well, if it's not your ex-husband and it's not somebody else, there's no reason why I shouldn't kiss you, is there?"

There were a hundred reasons why not, but they all escaped Lee at that moment as he tipped her face up once more. The noon sun sent splinters of light through minute openings in the branches overhead into their private domain, like miniature green-gold starbursts. Somewhere in the distance a meadowlark warbled.

"Brown, you're my boss and I don't think—"

His kiss cut off her argument as he leaned over, pressing a palm against the floor behind her, and meeting her lips above the brown paper bag and the remains of their meal. His lips were cold from the drink, but soft and appealing as he tipped his head to the side and moved it in lazy, seductive motions back and forth. The coolness left the skin of his inner lips and was replaced by warmth from her own.

Oh, Brown, Brown, you're too damn good at this.

Lee found her common sense at last and pulled back, but Sam continued leaning toward her in that nonchalant pose. The wrist and can were on his knee again, but his eyes were on her mouth.

"I've been thinking about that since long before our walk today," he said.

"Don't say things like that." She frowned at his chin to convince him she was serious, though she suspected she was the one who needed convincing for it had suddenly become very hard to breathe.

"Why not?" he asked with a half smile.

"Because it could cause innumerable problems, and I'm not up to handling them."

He leaned even closer. "No problems—I promise." While she was still trying to sort out rationality from response, he kissed her again, sending tiny shudders up her arms and fluid fire through her veins. His warm tongue circled her lips, and even as she told herself this was dangerous, this man was too appealing and far, far too expert, her lips parted and answered his tongue with a first hesitant response. The kiss grew warmer and wider and better until Sam Brown's softly sucking mouth melted Lee's resistance, and she leaned toward him, realizing how much—how very much—she had missed this.

Oh, Brown, we never should have started this.

But even as she thought it, his mouth left hers and she watched, mesmerized, as he slipped the can from her fingers and placed it to one side with his own. He confiscated her sandwich, which now wore two flat-pressed fingerprints. Methodically, he cleared away the rest of their lunch and placed the bag beside the soft drink cans on his far side. When he turned back to her, his intention was clear.

The pulse jumped in Lee's throat, and a band seemed to cinch about her chest, bringing with it a sweet expectation that rivaled the sweet scent of the orchard. Sam's right hand slipped to her ribs, his left to cup her hip and slide her over until she bumped firmly up against him. Then her head was tipping back and his warm lips opened over hers again.

A thousand forgotten feelings swept over Lee as Sam's hand slipped beneath the ribbing at her waist and her fingers found his collarbone. It had been so long . . . so long. Then, in one deft motion, he pulled her across his chest and took her backward with him, falling onto the bed of the pickup, little caring that it was hard and dirty and cold.

Her shirt slid up as his hand moved over her bare back and warm fingers slipped underneath the narrow band of elastic that crossed beneath her shoulder blades. His other hand slid down over her backside and expertly adjusted her length atop his own until she felt exactly how tough and hard all that running had made his thighs. And while he kissed and tempted her with a strong molding of tongue upon tongue, something more grew tough and hard beneath Lee's body. Her own body leaped to life.

And—oh, God—it felt so wonderful to be held again, caressed again. Sam's compelling lips shut out all thought of stopping the warm hand that curved around the side of her breast while his other arm pressed against her spine. He slipped his fingers inside the front of her bra, between lace and skin, the tips not quite reaching her nipple. A moment later he'd reached around her to release the clasp between her shoulder blades. His warm palms moved between their bodies, finding her freed breasts and caressing them slowly before rolling their tips between his fingers as if they were flowers he'd plucked on their stroll through the meadow.

He was ardent and persuasive and so undeniably tempting as she lay on him. She knew all the dangers of succumbing to his tantalizing sorcery, but she told herself not to think of them as her body responded fully.

But then Sam suddenly rolled her to her hip and reached for the snap on her jeans, and she plummeted to earth again.

"Brown . . . this is crazy, stop it!" She caught his straying hand and dragged it to safer territory. Everything inside her had gone zinging-singing, turned-on crazy with incredible desire for him. His eyes glinted down into hers like dark, metallic sparks, and his fingers curled into the back of her hand until she whispered fiercely, "Don't!"

To Lee's immense surprise and relief, he rolled away and fell flat on his back, his hands coming to rest, knuckles down on the corrugated metal beneath him.

"Sorry, Cherokee."

That name again! It did the strangest things to her

stomach. She sat up and drew a steadying breath, wondering what had ever possessed her to let things get so far out of hand. She was thoroughly embarrassed now, for even with her back to him she could feel his eyes on her. But she had little choice except to reach behind her for her bra.

Once again Sam Brown did the unpredictable. He sat up immediately and slipped his hands under her shirt. "Here, let me. I'm the one who messed it up." With a total lack of compunction he pushed her shirt up and found the trailing ends of the bra and hooked them together again. His putting it back on had an even greater sexual impact than when he'd released it. Goose bumps erupted over her skin and left her more tinglingly aware of him than ever. But he unselfconsciously pulled the shirt down to her waist, smoothed it into place, and dropped his hands from her. He seemed to dismiss the entire episode with an almost cheery note. "You're probably right. We should stop."

She was astonished by his mercurial change of mood. Somehow she'd expected him to be demanding or angry at her rebuff. But he sat beside her now as if they'd shared nothing more than a bag lunch. At least that was the impression he gave until his lopsided grin returned and he drawled devilishly, "But it *was* fun."

She bit back a smile and scolded, "Brown, have you no scruples whatsoever?"

"Well, I didn't see you exactly high-tailing it in the other direction."

"Oh no?" She boosted herself up and dropped off the tailgate, then turned to inform him from that safe distance, "I think it's time we headed back to town."

He only grinned, curled his hands over the edge of the tailgate, and swung his legs loosely from the knees.

"Whatcha doing this weekend, Cherokee?"

"Cut that out, Brown. I said I don't want problems."

"I've got another name besides Brown, you know."

"That's all we need—a little more familiarity between us, and everyone in the office will have their jaws wagging."

"What time do you get up on Saturdays?"

How was a woman supposed to fight an irresistible tease like him? It was all she could do to keep a straight face.

"None of your business. Are you coming or not?"

He leaped nimbly from the truck, revealing three dirty stripes down the back of his white shirt. As he slammed the tailgate shut he suggested, "How about we rent some roller skates and try the skate trails?"

"I said no!" She added in exasperation, "Oh, Lord, you're as striped as a polecat, Brown. Hold still while I get rid of the evidence."

She stepped quickly up behind him to whisk the

dirt away, but as her hands brushed over his hard back, he grinned over his shoulder—a devastatingly charming grin. "You scared I might make a pass at you again and catch you in a weaker moment?" She felt a telltale blush creep across her cheeks and immediately stepped back and jammed her hands into her pockets.

"You know what your problem is? You read too many girlie magazines!"

Sam laughed and plucked an apple off a tree, then draped his elbows on top of the tailgate behind him as he took a lazy bite.

"Well, I just thought, since you'd changed your brand of perfume—"

"That wasn't perfume, that was mosquito spray!"

Again his rich peal of appreciation lifted through the orchard before his teeth snapped through the skin of the apple. He considered her unhurriedly. "What about tomorrow?"

The man was undauntable. If he kept it up, he'd break her down yet! She stamped her foot and declared, "No, no, a thousand times no!" then spun from him, strode to the pickup, and got in.

He flung the apple core beneath the trees and climbed in beside her as she wondered frantically how to break the sexual tension spinning between them. But as Sam started the engine, he managed to break it himself by glancing at her from the corner of his eye and teasing, "You know, you're cuter 'n hell when you're on the warpath, Cherokee."

She could resist no longer and burst out laughing. He was an outlandish tease and a tempting creature. But he was her boss and the last man in the world she should encourage—assuming she wanted to encourage any man, which she didn't. Yet even as she promised herself sternly to avoid being alone with Sam Brown, a glow of well-being spread from her smiling lips all the way down to her tingling toes.

Chapter
SEVEN

LEE spent the following morning at her usual Saturday drudgery—cleaning house. She had changed the sheets, cleaned the upstairs, vacuumed the steps, and was shoving the vacuum cleaner along the living room carpet when she thought she'd heard the doorchime. She heard it again more clearly and, mumbling a curse, turned the machine off with a bare toe.

She opened her front door and stopped dead still. There, his hips against the wrought-iron handrail, sat Sam Brown, practically naked!

"Hi," he greeted, puffing hard. "This is an obscene house call."

Without warning, Lee burst out laughing. She covered her mouth with both hands and bent forward, overcome with mirth. "Oh, Brown, I believe you!"

There he sat, wearing nothing but his beat-up running shoes, a pair of white jogging shorts with a green stripe, and a red headband. Sweat ran down his heaving chest, making it shine in the sun. There was little hair on it, but what there was burned like red-gold sparks as trickles of perspiration ran down the center hollow toward his navel. His legs were crossed at the ankle, but his shoulders slumped forward as he panted laboriously.

"Don't tell me you ran all the way over here," Lee said.

He nodded, still trying to catch his breath.

"But it must be eight miles!"

"Eight mi . . . hiles is nothing. I'm in goo . . . hood shape."

"I can see that." And she could, in spite of his breathlessness. He looked like poured copper, wet and smooth and sleek and sculptured, the muscles of his legs as hard as an Olympian's, his shoulders glossy and well developed.

"Must've lost six pounds of sw . . . sweat on the way ov . . . over here though."

"I can see that, too."

He drew in a large gulp of air, his breathing growing even while he continued to slump against the rail.

"You wouldn't turn a man away thirsty, would you?"

"And risk a darn good job?" Lee returned impertinently. "Come on."

Sam boosted himself away from the railing and followed Lee inside, making her uncomfortably conscious of her bare feet and legs and the strip of exposed skin between her skimpy bandeau top of white stretch terry and the faded denim cutoffs with strings dangling down her legs. She resisted an urge to run a hand over the single coarse braid that fell down her back and was as frayed around the edges as her cutoffs. She led Sam along the short hall to the rear of the house, where the kitchen's sliding glass door stood open to her small, shady patio. He stood before it, hands on hips, letting the draft cool his sweating body, as she opened the refrigerator.

"Here." She moved behind him with two clinking glasses.

"Thanks."

"Let's go out on the patio where it's more comfortable." She slid the screen open, and he followed. There was only a single webbed lounge chair, and before he could protest, Lee plopped down on the concrete, facing the lounge chair with her legs crossed Indian fashion. "Have a seat," she said.

"No, here, you take—"

"Don't be silly. You're the one who just ran eight miles, not me. Anyway, the concrete is cool."

He shrugged, dropped into the lounge chair, took a sip of tea, and glanced around at her pots of bright red geraniums, asparagus fern, and vinca vine. It was cool and restful in the shade, but Lee felt warm and uncomfortable as Sam's eyes returned to her. What should she say to this man who refused to accept her brush-off and appeared at her door the next day with incorrigible brashness . . . then made her laugh!

"Do you run every day?"

"I try to."

"I don't think I'd care to on a day like today. It's supposed to get up to ninety-five degrees."

"That's why I run in the morning."

"Mmm." She sipped her drink, aware of his eyes, which made a periodic sweep of the geraniums but always returned to her bare knees.

"Did I interrupt something important?" He glanced toward the house, where the vacuum cleaner was sprawled across the living room floor.

"Just the weekly house cleaning." Lee grimaced, then added, "Ugh!"

Sam laughed, then the corners of his lips remained in a teasing grin. "Heap big disgusting job, cleaning the teepee?"

She couldn't stop her smile. "Show some respect, would you, Brown?"

"Well, you should see yourself"—he gestured with his glass—"sitting there barefooted with your legs crossed and that braid dangling down your back and your skin the color of a too ripe peach. The name Cherokee fits better than ever." He polished off the rest of his tea in one gulp and set the glass down, still grinning.

"You know"—she tipped her head to one side—"it puzzles me why I let you get away with it. If anybody else said things like that to me, I'd give 'em a black eye."

"You tried that once on me too, remember?"

"You deserved it."

He threw his head back, closed his eyes, and crossed his hands over his naked belly. "Yeah, I did."

How was a woman supposed to deal with a man like him? There he sat, as composed as a potentate, looking for all the world like he was going to take a nap on her patio.

"If you just stopped by to catch forty winks, do you mind if I finish my cleaning?"

He opened one eye. "Not at all." The eye closed again, and a moment later Lee slid the screen door open. The vacuum cleaner wheezed on, and for some reason she found herself smiling. She heard nothing more from Sam Brown until about fifteen minutes later, when she was watering the living room plants. He stepped inside and stopped in the hall behind her. "Would you mind if I used your bathroom before I head back?"

She turned to see him filling the living room door-way with his bare shoulders and chest. "It's upstairs, to your right."

He sprinted up the steps as she turned back to wa-tering the plants. But a moment later she remem-bered the open door to the extra bedroom and turned, ready to bolt up and close it before he emerged from the bathroom. But as she reached the bottom step, the door above clicked open and the muffled thud of his footsteps sounded across the hall, pausing momen-tarily while she backed up, listening, a hand pressed to her heart. Again his footseps neared, and she scur-ried out to the kitchen, where she was busily scouring the sink when he found her again.

"Thanks for the iced tea. I've got an eight-mile run yet, so I guess I'd better go."

She ran her hands under the water, grabbed a towel, and followed him idly toward the front door, conscious of a great reluctance to see him leave. They stepped out onto the sunny front stoop, and he moved down two steps, then turned as she leaned against the railing with the towel slung over her shoulder. "I'll see you Monday, Cherokee," he finally said. The sun lit his hair to russet and his skin to cop-per as he gazed up at her without making a move. In another minute he would turn and jog off across the city. And all of a sudden she couldn't let him go. "It's eighty-five degrees already. There's no need for you to run all the way home. I can give you a ride if you want."

"What about your house cleaning?"

"It's all done."

"In that case, I accept."

Her heart went light and happy. "Give me a minute to put on some decent clothes, okay?"

She'd already stepped through the front door when his question stopped her. "Do you have to?"

Over her shoulder she threw him a scolding expression, but he only raised his palms, shrugged, and grinned.

She returned shortly, dressed in white pedal pushers and a red spaghetti-strap top that bloused at the waist and just above her breasts. As her bare feet slapped down the steps, a pair of red canvas sandals swung jauntily from two fingers, and white feathers bounced in her ears. Sam was leaning against the back fender of her dusty Pinto. He nudged himself upright and opened her door, waiting while she got in.

When he was seated beside her, she put the car into reverse. "If I remember right," she said, "you live on Ward Parkway . . . in the family rattrap." She gave him a sidelong grin.

"Everybody's got to live somewhere."

He settled back for the ride, and fifteen minutes later Lee was following Sam's finger as it pointed toward the cobbled drive of a majestic, well-preserved mansion.

Cradling the wheel in her arms, she stared in undisguised awe. Realizing Sam hadn't moved, she turned to give him a sheepish grin, then gazed up the ivy-covered chimney of the enormous stucco tudor home. "Nice little rattrap you live in," she said wryly.

"Would you like to see it?"

"Are you kidding?"

"Mother's not home. She's out golfing." The mention of his mother made Lee quail momentarily, though she wanted very badly to go inside his home and see where he lived, how he lived.

He seemed to sense her hesitation and turned, resting a knee on the seat between them, an arm along its back. "I'd like very much to spend the day with you, Cherokee. What do you say we do the town? Anything at all—think of the craziest, most illogical things you've ever thought of doing, and we'll try every one of 'em. And no more of what happened in the orchard yesterday. That's a promise."

It was a promise she would not have extracted had the choice been left up to her. "I *work* for you! Doesn't it sound just a little . . . well . . ."

"Hell, is that all? You think that if we end up more than friends you'll lose your job if and when the romance is over?"

"Something like that. Or at least it'll be a lot more

strained when we bump into each other in the office every day."

Engaging creases crinkled the corners of his eyes. "Maybe I should fire you here and now so the problem doesn't arise."

"Brown, you're impossible." But she couldn't help smiling as she shook her head at his foolish reasoning. Yes, he was impossible. Impossible to resist, with his dark good looks and his engaging sense of humor. She thrust her worries aside and promised herself a day of carefree fun. She would laugh and return his bantering and teasing and accept the fact that she enjoyed his company immensely.

"Say yes," he coaxed.

She gave him a wry corner-of-the-eye smirk. "You gonna fire me if I don't?"

"No."

"Then, yes, damn you."

The house was all cool class with an open stairway that dropped from the biggest fanlight window Lee had ever seen. Sam ran upstairs, leaving her to look around while he took a quick shower and changed. She wandered from room to room, hands clasped behind her back as if afraid to touch what she wasn't supposed to. The living room had two enormous sets of fanlight doors opening onto a glass-walled sunroom that overlooked the side yard, where the Kansas City traditions had been sustained—lush

flower beds curving around ancient magnolia trees; a
small fountain spouting water from a cupid's ewer;
and wrought-iron benches enclosed on three sides by
precision-trimmed boxwood hedges.

"Ready?"

Lee turned to find that Sam had come up silently
behind her on the thick, white carpeting. He looked
as inviting as his house and yard. She forced her
eyes back to the luscious view outside. "I had no
idea," she murmured.

"It gets kind of lonely sometimes," he replied.

Again she turned. He was standing nearer,
smelling of fresh soap and that everlasting Rawhide
scent. His car keys were in his hand.

"Let's go get crazy," she said, giving him a devilish look meant to suggest just that.

THEY took the city by storm, skittering across it
like crazy bedbugs. Sam knew Kansas City well,
both its fun spots and its history, and he introduced
Lee to both. They rented roller skates and wheeled
through Loose Park, where the famed artist Christo
had once covered the sidewalks with shimmering gold
cloth and entitled his work "Wrapped Walkways."
They bought bandages at the drugstore and entitled
their works "Wrapped Knees." They bought a rhine-
stone ring at the Country Club Plaza and put it on

the finger of a fountain nymph in the Crown Center, declaring a bond forever between the two magnificent landmarks whose creators, Lee learned, had both had the initials J. C. They got separated in the midst of the colorful *Festa Italiana* in Crown Center Square and recovered each other from the arms of exuberant Italian dancers. They ate ice cream at Swenson's and drank piña coladas at Kelly's Saloon, then nearly lost both on the Zambezi Zinger at Worlds of Fun, and settled their stomachs by lying flat on their backs between rows of markers at Mount Washington Cemetery. They spit into the "Mighty Mo" off the middle of the Hannibal Bridge, with laughing apologies to Octave Chanute, who hadn't taken two and a half years creating it just to have two zanies use it for this! They slipped into the Truman Library and left a note commemorating the date in the *Encyclopedia Britannica*—in Volume 7, page 754—promising to come back a year from then and see if it was still there.

All day they walked along Kansas City streets named after the city's founders—Meyer, Swope, Armour. Sam showed Lee Kessler Boulevard, named after the landscape architect who'd mapped out the entire beautification system of boulevards, gardens, and fountains that made the city a splendid kaleidoscope of beauty. He told her the history of William Rockhill Nelson, the founder of the *Kansas City*

Star, who had fought for the city's approval of the unique boulevard network for fourteen years, and of how Jesse Clyde Nichols's visionary planning had brought sculpture, fountains, and art objects to the city's intersections. They scampered, carefree, through the sun-splashed Kansas City day, and when night fell and the lights of the fountains lit their lilting waters to ruby, emerald, and sapphire, Lee and Sam sat on the edge of one eating Moo Goo Gai Pan and fried rice from little white cardboard containers.

"How's your knee?" Sam asked.

Lee lifted it and checked the bandage and the dried blood on her white pedal pushers. "Still intact. Next time I won't let you talk me into doing three hundred sixty degree turns when I haven't been on skates in years."

He chuckled, but his eyes rested on her with a warm, appreciative glow.

"You're a helluva good sport, you know that, Cherokee?"

"Thanks. You ain't so bad yourself, Your Honor."

"You ready to call it a day?"

"Am I ever." She patted her stomach, sighed, then stacked the white cartons one inside the other. They meandered away from the fountain toward Sam's car, dropping their trash on the way . . . and somehow when he returned to her side, his hand took hers . . .

and somehow she didn't mind a bit. A few minutes later, as their wide-swinging steps moved more lazily, Sam Brown looped an arm around Lee's neck and drew her close to his side. It felt good to be there, so she lifted a hand and hung it from his wrist, watching their feet go slower and slower.

Sam drove leisurely through the Kansas City night, listening to the night sounds of crickets and frogs through the open windows. The fountains along Ward Parkway *shushed* past, and Lee rested her head against the seat, wishing the evening needn't end at all. Sam pulled up in his driveway and turned off the engine. Neither of them moved.

"Thanks for a really fun day," she said softly.

"The pleasure was mine."

Still neither of them moved.

"I see Mother's home. Would you like to meet her?"

"Not tonight. It's late . . . and I've got bloody knees and Moo Goo Gai Pan on my shirt." The very thought of meeting his mother threatened to flaw the perfect day.

Lee felt Sam studying her across the car seat, and a moment later his voice came quietly. "Cherokee?"

"Yes?"

He hesitated before saying, "There's no Moo Goo Gai Pan on your shirt." Immediately she reached for her door handle, but his hand came out to detain her.

"I'd really like you to meet my mother. Why are you running away?"

She laughed nervously and said to her lap, "I'm really not very good with mothers." She turned an entreating glance up at him and added softly, "I'd rather not."

His thumb moved softly, brushing the crook of her elbow. "Do you mind telling me why?"

She considered doing just that, then answered without rancor, "Yes, I do mind."

Disregarding her answer, he went on, "Let me guess. It's got something to do with your being part Indian."

She was stunned that he'd figured out that much of the truth and felt as if, for a moment, he'd looked into her very soul.

"H . . . how did you know?"

His eyes moved to the feathers at her ears and with a single finger he set one in motion, then explained, "You're very defensive about it, you know."

"Everybody wears Indian jewelry these days. It's very in."

"Don't get mad, Cherokee. It's been a great day, and I want to keep it that way. But I wish you'd level with me. So far you haven't told me much of anything about your past." A long pause followed before he encouraged softly, "Why don't you tell me now?"

She considered for a moment and realized she

wanted very badly to tell him. But it was hard to explain. It had been so long.

"I . . . I don't know where to begin."

"Begin with your husband. Was he white?"

"Yes." She dropped her eyes.

"And?"

"And . . ."

When she didn't go on, he urged softly, "Look at me, Cherokee. And what?"

His eyes were pools of shadow as he leaned across the dark confines of the car, and at the concern in his voice she suddenly found herself wanting to tell him things she'd promised herself never to reveal. But she needed to put some distance between herself and Sam Brown while she told him, so she opened her door and got out, leaving him to follow. As they ambled slowly toward her car, she began haltingly.

"Joel married me in one of those . . . those idiotic rebounds from the woman he should have married in the first place. A very white woman of whom his mother heartily approved. He'd . . . he'd had a fight with her, so when he met me it was . . ." She sighed and looked up at the stars. "Oh, I don't know what it was. A chemical mix-up, maybe. A stupid impulse. But we didn't think it out at all. We just did it. Too fast, too . . ." She shrugged and hugged her arms as they moved across damp grass. "Nothing about it was right, not from the very first, except maybe the sex.

But that's not enough to sustain a marriage. After a while his mother's disapproval of me began to wear on Joel, and he began blaming me for alienating him from his family. Within a year after our divorce, he married the girl his mother had been telling him all along he should have married." They stopped at her car. "So now you know why I'm not too good with mothers."

The lights from the house spilled in long white splashes across the dark lawn behind them. Sam stood with a hand in his trouser pocket. Lee waited for his response. When it came, she was pleasantly surprised. The hand came out of his pocket and captured her elbow and he spoke in a soft, cajoling voice.

"Now that that's out of the way, come here." His gentle grip swung her around to face him, then he looped his arms around her waist till their hips rested lightly against each other. And suddenly she forgot about mothers and personal histories, for Sam Brown's face was smiling down at her through the warm, flower-scented night. It seemed as if the beguiling fountains of Kansas City itself danced within Lee's heart as she waited for one thing she needed to make this day end in total perfection. Then he lowered soft, warm open lips over hers, and she lifted her own, slightly parted, readily accepting the brush of his tongue upon hers . . . but softly, gently.

Ah, Brown, the things you do inside me.

He held her lightly, only the tips of her breasts brushing his shirt while she rested her hands on his biceps. Sam's tongue stroked and coaxed, and Lee's answered, her fingertips slipped up beneath the ribbing of his short knit sleeves in an unconscious invasion of his firm, hidden skin. The kiss was unhurried, almost lazy, a sweet lingual blandishment while they leaned a little apart and began to rock indolently from side to side. It was an aperitif of a kiss, designed to whet the appetite for more. But when it ended—slowly, lingeringly—they refrained from partaking further.

Sam lifted his head to tease softly, "That's better than Swenson's ice cream."

Lee smiled and leaned back against the circle of his hands. "Mmm . . . and it won't give you a stomachache, either."

He smiled impishly and settled his hips more firmly against hers. "Oh no?"

But she knew it wasn't his stomach that ached. She could feel what ached, pressed hard and inviting against her pedal pushers.

So she was surprised when a moment later she found herself pushed gently away and turned toward her car by the Honorable Sam Brown, who was proving increasingly honorable indeed.

Chapter
EIGHT

Early Monday morning, plans got under way for bidding the Little Blue River job. Again Lee noted the difference between the way things were done at Brown & Brown and at Thorpe Construction. Not only was there an ongoing sense of cooperation where she worked now, but there was also a thoroughness that surprised her.

Accurate records of soil workability were kept for all major jobs. Lee met the drill truck on site Monday afternoon to take soil samples directly from the steel auger. These were weighed, dried, and run through a series of nested copper sieves. The amounts of material retained on each of the variously gauged screens were weighed carefully and recorded on a gradation chart. Lee and Sam worked side by side sieving and recording the data. They compared their findings with those of former jobs under similar soil conditions and used the results to estimate the cost of such variables as dewatering and sheeting to prevent cave-ins.

They sat in the coffee room, Frank perched on the edge of a counter, Sam seated with his legs crossed and heels propped up on an empty chair. The sense of belonging Lee felt in her new job encouraged her to take full part in the decision making. To her surprise her personal relationship with Sam hardly entered into their business dealings.

"Do you mind using Tri-State Drilling for dewatering?" Sam asked. His elbows were pointed at the ceiling and his fingers were clasped behind his neck as he leaned back comfortably.

"I was thinking of asking Griffin Wellpoint for a quote," Lee replied. "I've had good luck in dealing with them in the past." She held her breath. It was the first time she'd directly opposed the wishes of either Sam or Frank.

Sam only shrugged. "Great. We've had good luck with Tri-State, too, so either one is fine."

Lee ordered quotes from Griffin for dewatering, along with those from another subcontractor for installing pilings through the swampy area, which had proved to be mostly peat. She asked landscape contractors for quotes on sodding, seeding, mulching, and fertilizing. As the days passed and she waited for these quotes, the calculator on her desk whirred constantly.

She computed labor costs for pipe installation per foot, according to depth and soil conditions. Material costs were broken down into unit prices—and in the case of pipe, per-foot prices—and these extended out into lump sums.

As the week wore on and the day of the bid letting drew nearer, suppliers sent quotes on pipes, valves, manhole castings, and hydrants. Throughout the week the tension seemed to grow as bid day—Friday—approached. As usual, quotes from subcontractors came in late, holding up progress to some degree and lending a sense of uncertainty to the work on the bid.

Late Thursday, Sam stopped by Lee's desk and asked, "Have all those quotes come in from the subs yet?"

"Still waiting on one from Greenway. You know how it is."

He chuckled, but the sound seemed tense for Sam, who was usually relaxed and easygoing. "Yeah, I know how it is."

"You want this job badly, don't you?"

His eyes met Lee's and for the first time that week seemed to convey thoughts beyond soil evaluations and price per linear foot. "I've got a rather personal stake in this one. Don't you?"

Thoughts of the orchard in all its seductive glory came back. "Yes, I do."

He gazed down at her for a moment longer, then seemed to drag himself from his reverie to scratch the side of his neck and glance at the pale green job sheets draped across her desk. "Anyway, we could use this job since the Denver one doesn't get rolling till spring. There'd be time enough to get this one finished before winter."

Friday morning brought the usual eleventh-hour craziness Lee had come to expect in estimating. Somehow the spirit of competition never seemed to surface in suppliers until just before bid time. Within two hours of the deadline Lee received a call from the pipe supplier who was lowering his quote by twelve thousand dollars. Immediately subtotals and totals had to be changed on the official proposal form. Since the call came at 11:30 with bid time set for 2:00, Lee skipped lunch to change the figures, then run another calculator check of the math.

Sam came in at 12:45 to find her at her desk, her fingers flying over the machine, her bare feet curled up on the caster guards of her desk chair. "How's it going?" he asked.

She scarcely looked up. "What time is it?"

"Quarter to one."

"Will you double-check the addition on these sheets?"

"Sure." She extended the sheets without even turning her eyes his way. "Didn't you have lunch?"

She did glance up then, for about a half second. "No. American Pipe called and lowered their bid by twelve thousand dollars."

Sam sat down hastily at a nearby desk and his fingers, too, started flying over a calculator. "Why didn't you say something?"

She paused, looked up, and smiled at his dark head. "I'm too tense to eat anyway."

He pushed the total button, the machine clicked into silence, and Sam smiled across at Lee. "Relax, Cherokee, it's just a damn job."

But it wasn't, and they both knew it. It was *their* job. Their first joint effort, and something inside of Lee said they just had to win it! Still, she appreciated Sam's effort to put her at ease, and her smile said as much before they both set to work again.

Fifteen minutes later the changes were all entered in ink on the official bid proposal, and Sam leaned over Lee's desk to initial each one and put his signature beside the company seal impressed on the final sheet. His shoulder was almost touching her jaw as he bent to scratch his name on the paper. During the week, she'd had little trouble controlling personal feelings that intruded during business hours, but now, as he stood close and she watched his dark hands moving on the white paper, she was drawn to him by their singularity of purpose. He dropped the pen, straightened, and smiled down at her feet.

"You can put your shoes back on now. It's done."

She grinned sheepishly. "Takes the pressure off the head."

"Maybe off yours, but not off mine." He gave her feet an appreciative grin just as a group of draftsmen returned from lunch. "Well, I'm holding you up, huh?" It was one o'clock, and she still had to drive clear across the city to the Independence City Hall.

She drew in a deep breath, raked a hand through her hair, and gave Sam a shaky smile. "Well, here goes."

Brown & Brown's new estimator gathered up her papers, slipped the bid into a large gold envelope, licked it, pressed it shut, and lifted her eyes to find that her boss had been watching her every move.

"Good luck, Cherokee," he said softly.

"Thanks, Your Honor," she returned. Then she slipped on her shoes, picked up her purse, and left the office.

BROWN & Brown took the Little Blue River job for $750,000, only $7,900 below the next highest bidder. When the last bid was read and the announcement made, Lee felt adrenaline swoop into her bloodstream in a giddy swoosh. She rose to her feet to accept handshakes, and her knees felt wobbly and weak. Her palms had been sweating throughout the opening of the envelopes, but now they itched to get to a telephone and call the office.

She suffered through what seemed like hours of felicitations before finally escaping to the pay phone in the hall.

Rachael's perky voice answered, "Brown & Brown."

"Rachael, we got it!" Lee announced without prelude.

"Lee! That's wonderful!"

"Isn't it, though?" Lee bubbled. "I'm ecstatic . . . and a little shaky."

Rachael laughed. "That part never changes, honey."

A little chuckle released the last of her nervousness, then Lee requested, "Put Sam on, will you, Rachael?"

She listened to the silence on the line for a brief moment, basking in a deep sense of satisfaction as she waited for his voice. When it came, it sounded full of smiles.

"Nice going, Cherokee."

"Hallelujah, we did it, Brown!"

He laughed. "Feels good, huh?"

"Does it ever."

"Just how good?"

Understanding his cryptic question, she replied, "Only seventy-nine hundred dollars good . . . that's how good."

"You mean that's all you left!"

"Yes!"

At his laugh of satisfaction, Lee pictured the smile carving grooves into his cheeks and the pale laugh lines disappearing about his eyes.

"Who came in second?"

"Just a minute, I'll read you the list."

She relayed the remainder of the bids, then Sam asked, "You're coming back to the office, aren't you? We've got to celebrate your first victory."

"I'll be there in an hour or so."

"Good, see you then."

In the business of estimating, the days of defeat far outnumbered those of victory. On winning days, a special elation seeped into everyone, creating a spirit of camaraderie and good humor. Coming back into the office to find that everyone in the house had already heard the good news, Lee stopped to accept congratulations and share lighthearted jokes with her coworkers. But one was foremost in her mind.

Sam was beaming as he strode across the blue carpet dressed in casual gray slacks and a pale blue dress shirt with the sleeves rolled up to the elbow. Lord, she'd never been as proud as she was then, facing Sam Brown. Her smile was infectious as he extended his wide hand and clasped hers, squeezing hard, shaking it just once, and holding it only a fraction of a second longer than necessary.

"Congratulations, Lee."

"Thank you, Sam." She wished she could lay her other hand over his and tell him how much she'd appreciated his faith in her during the past week, and what a true pleasure it had been preparing the bid in the congenial atmosphere of his office, among his cooperative employees and—of course—with him. But his hand slipped away, and the group of men continued chattering. Rachael, Nelda, and Ron Chen joined the group, and to Lee it felt like Christmas Eve.

Some people were already clearing off their tables, others still standing around shooting the breeze, when Rachael pulled herself away from a drafting table and turned toward the front. "Well, hi, Mary, how are you?"

A darkly tanned woman of about sixty had entered the office and was moving familiarly toward the cluster of men and women. Most of them greeted her by name and exchanged anecdotal greetings. Obviously they all knew her. She was dressed in a classy looking summer suit with brown and white spectator pumps and a matching purse. She exuded an air of quiet confidence.

"I understand congratulations are in order around here," she commented as she approached.

To Lee's amazement, Sam broke away from the others and greeted the woman with a light kiss on the cheek.

"Hi, Mother. You out slumming?" he teased.

"I heard the news. Thought it was time I met your new estimator."

"She's right here." Sam looped an arm around his mother's shoulder and directed her toward Lee, who stood stock still with amazement.

"Mother, this is Lee Walker—Lee, my mother, Mary Brown." He had placed his hands on his mother's shoulders, and his dark, amused eyes twinkled down at Lee as color rose to her cheeks. Like a robot she extended her hand, which was clasped in very dark, coppery fingers with wide knuckles and several flashy diamonds.

"I'm happy to meet you, Mrs. Brown," Lee managed, unable to keep her eyes from fleeing back to Sam, who stood as before, with his hands on his mother's shoulders, an undisguised look of merriment crinkling the corners of his eyes.

"So you've won your first bid for Brown and Brown," the woman noted in a friendly fashion as she studied Lee from a face with wide, high cheekbones and a blunt, broad nose. Her hair was graying now, but was unmistakably coal black underneath the lighter strands.

"I . . . uh . . . yes, but not alone. Frank and . . . and your son worked with me on it."

"Sam wanted it quite badly. He mentioned it several times this week. Well, congratulations." She smiled, then added, "And welcome to the company."

As Sam's hands fell from her shoulders, he grinned disarmingly at Lee, then turned to watch his mother visit with others before joining her. Just then the phone rang. One of the draftsmen picked it up.

"It's for you, Lee."

It was a salesman asking if she'd go out for a drink or dinner—standard procedure after winning a bid. The salesmen were always eager to write up orders. Lee was standing with her back to the room when she suddenly became aware that Sam had slipped quietly up behind her. She turned, glancing at him over her shoulder as she spoke into the receiver. "This afternoon?" She paused for the salesman's reply, then asked, "What time?" With the phone pressed to her ear, Lee watched Sam Brown reach for a pad and pencil and followed his movements as he wrote, "You owe me dinner . . ." He turned it her way and pierced her with a meaningful look as she tried valiantly to concentrate on what the voice on the phone was saying. Sam's hand moved again, adding, ". . . tonight." He punctuated the message with an exclamation point.

Lee turned her back on both Sam Brown and his message, stammering, "Ah . . . I'm sorry, Paul, what were you saying?" A quick glance over her shoulder told her that Sam had moved away again. "I'm sorry, Paul. Maybe we can make it Monday for lunch. I'm busy tonight."

They made arrangements to meet then, and by the time Lee hung up, the office was starting to empty. She looked around for Sam's mother, but found she had gone. Sam himself was coming toward Lee. She crossed her arms loosely over her chest and leaned against the desk as she watched him approach.

"Well, you've surprised me again, Your Honor." Lee smiled.

"Have I now?" His grin was utterly charming.

"You know perfectly well that you have. Your mother is more Indian than I am."

"Ah, you're very perceptive," he teased.

"Where is she?" Lee scanned the office again.

Sam shrugged, then smirked. "Probably gone home to clean the teepee."

A picture of his "teepee" flashed before Lee's mind, and she couldn't help laughing. "Sam Brown, you're impossible. Why didn't you tell me before this?"

"And let you stop thinking I hired you so I could become a minority contractor? I've had too much fun laughing about it to myself."

"At my expense?"

"It didn't cost you anything, did it?"

"Except my unflappable cool. I think you could've driven a front-end loader in my mouth when I got a look at her and realized she was your mother."

He smiled, but changed the subject abruptly. "What about that dinner?"

She cocked an eyebrow at him. "I take it you're holding me to my promise that I go out with you when I became low bidder."

"Exactly."

"And I *am* low bidder?"

"Yes you are."

"And I *do* keep my promises?"

His smile broadened. "I'll pick you up at your place at seven. Wear something dressy." He turned away, changed his mind, and returned momentarily to add, "And sexy." Then he left for good.

LEE chose white again—this time a sleek, lithe crepe de chine dress that slipped over her hips like water—not tight, not loose, but willowy. It was a simple cylinder, cinched by elastic above her breasts and at the waist, leaving her shoulders and upper chest bare, the perfect foil for a heavy turquoise and silver pendant shaped like a peyote bird that dropped onto her chest from a silvery chain. She touched it

and looked at her reflection in the mirror, remembering Sam Brown's mother. How like him not to tell her
the truth, then let her find it out as she had. She
smiled, then hurried to insert tiny droplets of dangling turquoise in her ears. On her feet went the
briefest straps of white leather and high, high heels.
She tricked her hair into a froth of sassy curls, their
disheveled control confined only by a fine white headband that crossed her temples and disappeared amid
the bouncy tangle on her head.

Just then the doorbell rang. Without thinking, Lee
snatched the framed picture of her sons from the
dresser top and stuffed it into a drawer. On her way
out she took a moment to close the door to the second
bedroom. Downstairs she paused and pressed a hand
against her churning stomach, then took a deep breath
and went to greet Sam Brown.

He was leaning against the railing again, but he
seemed to unfold in slow motion, coming up off the
wrought iron muscle by muscle. As his ankles un-
crossed, as his hand came out of his trouser pocket,
as he pulled himself to his feet, his eyes shimmered
down the length of Lee, and a smile of undisguised
appreciation lifted his sculptured lips. When his dark
eyes met her even darker ones, he said flat out, "You
look absolutely sensational, Cherokee."

His approval brought a sweet ripple of pride up

her spine as she took in the crisp lapels of his navy blue suit.

"Thank you, Your Honor, so do you." Did he ever! His white shirt set off the rusty hue of his face like a well-chosen matting about a painting, and she wondered how she could have been so naive as to have missed the truth about his heritage all this time. Yet from the first, she'd realized he didn't look like any full-blooded Scandinavian she'd ever known. He'd had his fun with her . . . but now, studying him, she couldn't help rejoicing at the final outcome. Yes, he was stunning, his silk tie knotted so flawlessly that it stood away from his collar band as if aroused.

At the thought she dropped her eyes and turned to fetch a tiny beaded purse.

When he'd seen her solicitously to her side of the car and started the engine, he turned to study her again. She met his gaze levelly, unconcerned that he was undoubtedly reading the admiration in her perusal, just as she was in his.

"Tonight it's the American. I, too, keep my promises."

"But it was supposed to be my treat." She knew she couldn't afford the American Restaurant.

"Oh, you're wrong about that."

"But—"

"It's a company dinner, on the boss. I'll write it off as a business expense."

"Oh, in that case . . . the American it is." But Lee felt far removed from business concerns at the moment. And as the evening progressed, that distance widened.

THEY approached the Crown Center by way of its ten-acre square of terraced lawns and fountains, passing the massive tent pavilion and the thirty-foot-high umbrellas beneath whose yellow peaks they'd lost and found each other last Saturday. Alexander Calder's stabile "Shiva" loomed up before them, and minutes later they were entering the luxurious Westin Crown Center Hotel.

Its multilevel lobby was carved into a rocky hillside of natural limestone, creating a dramatic garden of tropical foliage and full grown trees through which tumbled a sixty-foot waterfall. The rushing water created a refreshing background music for hotel guests, shoppers from the adjacent Crown Center shops, and sightseers who sauntered along the elevated catwalks above the lobby.

Had Hans Christian Andersen been alive to dream up a fairy tale setting, he could not have invented any more compellingly romantic than that through which they passed, Lee thought. She found it difficult to keep her eyes from Sam, and when they found themselves the only two people on the elevator carrying them up to the restaurant, she gave in to the urge.

He was leaning against the left wall, she against the right. They studied each other wordlessly, caught up in a sense of impending intimacy. Horizons lay ahead for them—it seemed understood—which would change their relationship forever. The knowledge intensified the moment, though to all outward appearances they were as casual as before.

Lee's senses seemed honed to a fine edge. She was keenly attuned to Sam's familiar scent, to his expression which grew more and more thoughtful and sexually aware as the night wore on. Seated in the restaurant's lofty expanse with chrome and mirrors at her elbow and Kansas City spread out before her, Lee watched cars follow the arteries leading northeast toward the heart of the city. Yet time and again her gaze was pulled back to Sam's. As if her consciousness had been fine tuned, she absorbed every detail around her with acute perception—the soft hiss of bubbles in her stemglass; the sleek texture of pickled mushrooms from the toothpick Sam teasingly held toward her; the brush of his pant leg against her bare ankle under the table; the bite of woven caning against her bare shoulders as she relaxed in her bentwood chair; the heat of the flame from their Steak Diane as the waiter performed his culinary act; the sharp, tangy taste of broccoli, suddenly delectable when she'd never liked it before; the scent of starch in linen as she wiped her lips, which grew impatient for what now seemed a certainty; the sluggardly passage of time as Sam drew out their anticipation by ordering Cherries Jubilee; the flash of fire as a match was struck to liqueur; Sam's lips, tipped up only slightly at the corner as he slipped a scarlet cherry from a spoon and gave her a glimpse of his tongue stroking the succulent sauce from it; the heat flooding her body at his wordless suggestion.

Lee lounged all willowy in her chair, but she noted how often Sam's glance fell to the ruched line where her dress met her chest, then lower to the discernible shadows hinting of dusky, bare nipples within her silken bodice. Each time it happened her stomach tingled. But she lounged on, playing his waiting game with a restraint that keyed their sensuality to a higher pitch.

From the restaurant, across the square, to the car, and all the way home . . . he never touched her. Not with his hands. But his eyes were as tactile as the brush of warm flesh as they lingered on her. The city was dark, alive, waiting . . . just like Lee.

At the curb in front of her house the engine stopped and his car door opened, then he opened her door and waited for her to step out. Again they moved up the sidewalk, up the steps to the door without a word, without a touch.

She had left the outside light off. The shrubbery and overhanging roof created deep shadows. Yet she turned to him, knowing his face without seeing it.

"Would you like to come in for a drink?" She remembered his preference for dry martinis with pickled mushrooms and added nervously, "I . . . I don't have any pickled mushrooms, but I do have olives."

A long, blank pause followed before he replied succinctly, "No, I wouldn't care for a drink or pickled mushrooms or olives."

Her stomach trembled, and she drew in a deep breath before asking softly, "What, then?"

She sensed him leaning toward her, just short of touching her as he answered in a husky voice, "I want you, Cherokee . . . you know that."

His answer sent her pulse pounding, and suddenly she didn't know what to say. She stood there in the dark, her nostrils filled with his scent, knowing the searching look in his eyes, though she could not see them. Then his voice came again, soft but intense. "Don't invite me in unless it's for that."

Still he didn't touch her, and though she wanted him to, she knew that once he did there'd be no turning back.

"You must know I still have reservations about it," she admitted shakily.

"Then why did you wear that dress tonight with nothing under it?"

He knew her better than she knew herself; it seemed foolish to deny it. She dropped her chin and admitted artlessly, "It was shameless of me, wasn't it?" She sensed him smiling in the dark doorway.

"Are you testing me, Cherokee, to see how far you can go before I make a move?"

"No . . . I . . ." Her hands fluttered and her voice grew unsteady. "I'm just nervous."

After a thoughtful silence, he mused, "You're an enigma, you know that? I've seen you in action at a bid letting where there's a good reason to be nervous, yet there you're as unruffled as can be. Out in the tough business world you scrap and fight with the best of 'em. But what happens to that confident woman when a man finds her attractive?" His voice went softer. "What do you have to be nervous about?"

Suddenly there were tens of answers Lee could have given, any one of which would have been enough to stop her. But she withheld them all, realizing it had been half her doing that they were here together on the brink of something that would be splendid, she was certain. She did want him, and complications always went along with that, thus she suppressed her doubts and asked in a wistful way he could not mistake, "Would you like to come in for nothing so simple as . . . as pickled mushrooms or olives?"

In answer he reached out and gave her bare shoulder a brief squeeze that sent goosebumps down her arm.

"Give me your key," he ordered quietly.

Her hand trembled as she forfeited it. It chinked into his hand and a moment later the door swung inward, then closed behind them, securing them in a blanket of blackness.

She came to a halt in the middle of the hall, her back to Sam as she clutched her tiny purse in both hands. Oh, it had been so different with that other man, the one whose name she could barely remember, who had come oh so briefly after Joel. But she hadn't forgotten the sudden chill that had overcome her body and turned it unwilling at the last minute. What if that happened now? And what if . . . what if . . .

She ran a frenzied mental assessment of her body and found only its shortcomings—not only the stretchmarks but also the loss of firmness, the unmistakable contour of hips that were wider now, the few extra pounds she perhaps should have lost . . . and there was a single vein on . . .

Sam's hands sought her waist in the dark, and his fingers spread wide on her ribs, pulling her against him as he pressed his mouth into the curve of her neck, riding it back along the warm silver chain, pushing her hair aside to kiss the nape of her neck.

"Cherokee," he murmured, "you're so tense. There's no need to be."

In the dark he found the purse she still clutched and pulled it from her fingers. She heard the soft thud as it landed on a carpeted step before he returned his attentions to her neck.

She released the breath she'd held captive for too long and forced the muscles of her neck to relax one by one as he nuzzled the warm hollow behind her ear until her head dropped forward, then to the side.

"How long has it been?" he asked with gruff tenderness.

She knew a moment of trepidation before answering honestly, "Three years." Three long, empty years.

At her answer he circled her with both arms, just below her breasts, and she covered the sleeves of his suit jacket with her own arms and the backs of his hands with hers.

"You mean I'm the first since your husband?" he asked softly near her temple.

She swallowed thickly, then admitted, "Yes . . . no . . . well, almost."

She felt him move as if to look down at her questioningly, but his arms remained as before, warm and secure about her midriff.

"Almost?"

"There was one other man. I was lonely and . . ." Again she swallowed, thinking he'd pull away if she admitted what had happened. "Well, I thought I could, but . . . when I changed my mind things got ugly."

His arms tightened more firmly around her, and he rocked her soothingly a time or two. "Oh, Cherokee, can't you feel that's not going to happen to us?"

And suddenly she could. She relaxed against him as he wet the soft skin of her neck with the tip of his tongue and slipped a hand over her left breast, warm and resilient within the tissue-fine fabric of her dress. Shudders of pleasure made her skin prickle. Doubts fled magically. She no longer remembered that the skin he touched was not as firm as it had once been. She only reveled in how good it felt to be caressed again. She closed her eyes, and braved the question she, too, needed to have answered.

"How long has it been for you?"

His hand continued its gentle exploration even as he told her, "Three months."

"With who?"

The hand stilled on her breast. "Does it matter?"

"If she still means something to you, it does."

"She doesn't."

She relaxed even further, relieved more than she could say by his answer. The crepe dress seemed to have no more substance than a cobweb as he cupped his wide palms about the lower swell of both breasts and made the fabric slip seductively across her nipples, tempting them, making her insecurities retreat farther and farther, replacing them with the vast need to be touched again, fondled, loved.

"Oh, Cherokee, you feel so good," he murmured against her naked shoulder, dropping his head forward and crushing her back against him.

"So do you." She covered his hands and pressed them firmly against her breasts as if to absorb every nuance of tenderness. The wide palms moved beneath her hands, gentling and arousing at once, appeasing the need for quiet exploration. "Oh, Brown," she admitted breathily, "I've needed this for so long."

"I know," came his gruff voice beside her ear. "We all do." Then his fingertips familiarized themselves with the belled shapes of her nipples. He folded them between his thumbs and the edges of his hands, lifting her breasts at the same time, sending tiny tuggings of ache feathering along her nerves.

She hardly realized she'd sighed until his voice whispered in the hair above her ear, "That's better, Cherokee . . . relax."

And she was—oh, she was—for his hands seemed to stroke away her lingering misgivings, and the easy pace he'd set won her trust. His hands were very hard, both front and back, yet their touch was sensitive, and she made no effort to stop one from escaping her light hold. It slid over her stomach, where the fingers spread wide for a moment, then closed again before pressing into the hollow beside her hip. His touch became feather light as with a single fingertip he scribed a twining grapevine upon the mound of femininity within her silken skirt. He sent a perceptible shiver through her, for his movement over the crepe made it slip across equally silky undergarments until the sleek touch of her clothing sent ripples of sensuality up her spine. It made her powerfully aware of her own sexuality, this touch that was half caress, half tickle, and all arousal. She sensed him gauging her reaction, listening to the accelerated beat of her heart, feeling it beneath the palm that still pleasured her breast. At last he slipped his hand fully over the curve of her femininity, bringing her to know a wild rapture, a lush awakening.

He murmured her name—Lee, and sometimes Cherokee—kissing her ear, her jaw, her shoulder, as his hands rustled over her, learning her contours, then traveling once more up her stomach and sides until his thumbs hooked the elastic at the top of her dress, taking it down to her waist and freeing her breasts to his palms, which lingered only momentarily before one slipped low within her garments to touch her intimately for the first time. His voice was ragged as he uttered, "Oh, Cherokee, I've wanted this since the first night I saw you in that motel room."

She smiled in the dark thinking back to that night, realizing she'd been fighting a losing battle ever since. "I . . . I tried not to think of you, but it . . . it was impossible after that."

His touch drove the breath from her lungs and set her pulse thrumming, while behind her his body invited with its pressure, then with a faint side to side movement. But it was far easier to accept the first touch than bestow it. As if sensing her hesitancy, he rested his jaw against her temple and encouraged, "You know, you don't have to ask permission if there's anything you feel like doing."

Was he teasing? Only a little, and in an engaging way that sent a new awareness through her body. Yet girlish uncertainty mingled with womanly yearning. His midsection pressed firmly against her backside, verifying the message in his words while she hesitated yet a moment longer.

Then he begged softly, "Please, Cherokee . . ."

At last she drew her arm back, circling behind him to rest upon the tail of his suit jacket. His hand fell still upon her body, and his breath beat harshly against her ear as he waited . . . waited.

It had been so long . . . so long. But during these moments of sweet expectation she realized this intimacy had almost been predestined, for she and Sam had felt that spark from the first, and since then they had revealed bits and pieces of each other in the hope that each would find something more substantial to bring to his act. And now it was here, and her turn had come.

Her hand moved tentatively between them, and Sam backed away, giving her space and the right to know him. Her heart was like a wild thing in her breast as she touched him for the first time, a tentative caress that brought a strange, thick sound from his throat. She explored him through tailored gabardine until he lost the power to remain still beneath her fingers and ordered gruffly, "Turn around, Cherokee." Suddenly she was spun about by her shoulders, and her arms were lifting while their open mouths met like a crashing of worlds. She pressed her willing body against his, circling his neck, losing her fingers in thick hair at the back of his head, and exploring the contour of his skull before she felt herself being lifted off her feet.

"Your shoes . . ." he ordered against her lips.

Her toes worked the straps off her heels, as first one clunk sounded behind her, then another. A moment later her bare feet rested again on the cool tile floor, and his palms slid within the elastic at her waist, passing along her lower back. Down went the skirt, and with it pantyhose and silky briefs, to form a pool of fabric at her feet. He encircled her with powerful arms, lifted her off the floor for a second time, and kicked the garments aside. Another drugging kiss stretched into an abandoned celebration of discovery while hands, mouths, and hips paid homage. When he lifted his head a long time later, he asked hoarsely, "How do you feel about undressing a man?"

Perhaps it was then that she realized she could easily fall in love with Sam Brown, with this sensitive man who made it all so easy and kissed away the last remaining doubt.

She smiled and replied throatily, "Turn me loose and I'll show you."

The pressure fell away, and she slipped her hands under his jacket. Before it hit the floor she was working the knot of his tie from side to side. It joined the jacket. As he unbuttoned his cuffs, his forearms softly brushed her breasts, and his voice came low and husky and certain. "We're going to be good together, Cherokee. I just know it."

At that moment she knew it too, and she reached for his shirttails and pulled them free of his trousers.

She did it all, all that he wanted of her, removing each article of clothing with a newfound sense of freedom. And when he too was naked and reaching, her hips were taken firmly against his once more. Her fingertips found his bare chest, and she raised up on tiptoe to settle her bare breasts securely against it, and he ran his palms over her back.

He asked only a single word. "Where?"

"In the living room," she murmured against his

mouth before she was turned around and pulled back against his naked thighs while his legs nudged hers and they made their way onto soft, plush carpeting. She felt the pressure of his lips against her shoulder and answered their tacit command by bending with him. As they knelt, with one of his knees between hers, he aroused her with a magical touch until she lost all sense of time and drifted into a sensual paradise where a three-year void was eradicated by his knowing hands. The heat came slowly, starting in her toes, up her legs, along her flanks until her head pressed back against his shoulder and waves of pleasure broke across her skin.

She groaned, a strangled sound of abandon, and he clamped a steadying arm just below her breasts, holding her tightly against him while bringing her again the sense of self she'd lost somewhere along the years.

Behind her he was tense and rigid as his fingers curled into her shoulders, and a moment later she was turned and lowered quickly to her back and spread-eagled against the soft living room carpet.

It was a wild, primitive act they shared this first time, as if neither could control the tempo or the pressure. Celibacy had given Lee a need to match Sam's, so neither was concerned about the way they displayed their wantonness. It happened, as it was meant to happen, in an elemental and satisfying way neither had planned or anticipated. And when it was over and he fell heavily across her, they knew they'd shared something exceptional, even rare.

"Cherokee . . ." was all he could find the breath to say, but the single word was an accolade.

"Your Honor . . ." In other times, other contexts, the title had taken on a note of teasing, but now it was a sigh.

"You're wonderful," he praised.

"So are you . . . and . . . different than I expected."

He braced up, though his weight still pinned her lower half. "And what did you expect?"

"I . . . I don't know." With both hands she soothed the damp hair from his temples. Though it was still dark, her eyes had adjusted to the dimness, and she could discern the outlines of his features. "All I know is I was very unsure, and . . . and feeling rather inadequate, and you made me forget all that."

He ran an index finger along the rim of her nose. "Inadequate? Why?"

How foolish it seemed now, yet minutes ago she had felt uncertain. "The second time a woman loses the confidence that comes so easily with the first time."

He kissed the tip of her nose with exquisite tenderness. "You're anything but inadequate, Cherokee. But in case you still have doubts, I'm volunteering to do my best to soothe them—indefinitely."

She tried to chuckle, but it was hard with his weight pressing the air from her lungs. She settled comfortably at his side and lay with her head on his arm while his hand rested on her hip.

She had forgotten the deep lethargy and satisfying afterglow of love. She basked in it now, resting in the curve of his arm, cherishing this lazy time which was the antithesis of what had just passed, but equally as necessary.

She curled up even more securely against his side, listening to the thud of his heart against her ear and running a finger from the corner of his lips to the soft center. His kissed her finger, which slipped into the moist, lush interior of his mouth before he bit it very gently, then continued holding it between his teeth.

Ruminating on the minutes just past, she murmured, "That was terrible, wasn't it?"

"What was so terrible about it?"

"Uninhibited," she mumbled, slightly chagrined at the memory.

"Are you saying you want to take it a little slower next time?"

"Next time?" She reached up and playfully yanked a handful of his hair. "You certainly take a lot for granted."

"Oh, do I now?" He rolled her on top of him and settled her along his length, then ran his hands down her spine until his fingertips touched a part of her that disproved her words. And when they'd shared another ripple of mirth, he wrapped his arms around her securely and kissed her cheek.

"Cherokee, you're all woman, and you're more than enough to suit me. Mind if I hang around for a while?"

"Mmm . . . how long did you have in mind?"

"Oh . . . till morning, anyway." She heard the grin in his words, which brought a corresponding smile to her own lips.

But though she smiled and teased, "That long, huh?" the thought of morning was something to be reckoned with. Morning, with its bright revealing sun. She nudged the thought away, nestling against him, wanting him beside her throughout the night.

Morning would take care of itself.

Chapter
NINE

LEE watched dawn creep into the bedroom, all coral and cozy, illuminating their two bodies beneath strewn sheets, she on her belly, Sam on his back. Her eyes followed the brown and white cat that padded into the room, stopped beside the window where it lifted its nose to sniff the cool morning air, puffing the draperies gently from the sill, tapping the plastic bell on the end of the pull. Nose to the air, the cat stood for long minutes, then bounded onto the bed, landing in a most unfortunate spot.

Sam came up like a jack-in-the-box, uttering a sharp cry of surprise followed by an expletive. The cat went flying through the air like a missile as Lee braced up on both palms to observe Sam tenderly massaging his abused parts through the sheets.

She fell onto her belly again, chuckling into the pillow. "What's the matter? Was I too hard on you last night?"

"What the hell was that!"

"That was my cat, P. Ewing."

"Ohhh," he groaned. "I thought the bed was booby-trapped."

She laughed silently, hugged the pillow beneath one cheek, and peered up at him. "Can I help?"

He turned his head, all tousled and dark, and amusement curved his lips. "Your damn cat just . . . just pickled my mushrooms, woman, and you lie there making jokes?" It appeared he'd forgotten his discomforts now. He folded his arms behind his head and closed his eyes. "Don't talk to me, I'm pouting." But the corners of his lips twitched.

Lee studied him at leisure, noting that his beard had grown overnight, that his chest was wide and dark, that his nipples were the color of rosebuds. Pleasure came wafting over her at waking to the sight of such a man in her bed. He was as handsome as he was entertaining, and she let her eyes linger on his lips, brows, and eyelashes. She reached out and ran the tip of a fingernail just inside the rim of his nostril.

"Oh, Bro-o-w-wn?" she sing-songed seductively, going up and down the scale.

His nose twitched, but his eyes remained closed.

"Oh, Brow-w-wn . . ." she crooned again, tickling the edge of his other nostril. He wriggled his nose, then rubbed it distractedly before crossing his arms behind his head as before, with eyes still closed. She shimmied over beside him, propped her bare breasts coquettishly on his chest, and rested her chin on crossed wrists.

"Hey, Brown, you were right, this bed is booby-trapped. Wanna see?"

His chest shook silently, but he lay as before.

"Hmm?" she teased.

"Naw."

She snickered, unable to keep a straight face any longer. He opened one eye and looked down his nose at her.

"But I've got something here you might be interested in witnessing," he said.

"What's that?"

"A genuine Indian uprising."

They were dissolved by paroxysms of laughter then, even as his powerful arms closed around her and flipped her over. They shared a first good morning kiss, but before it ended the laughter had faded away. Lee held his face in both hands and said in a husky tone, "Oh, Brown, you're so good for me."

His ebony eyes ran over her face, touching her lips, nose, and tousled hair before meeting her own eyes.

"Lee," he requested in a strangely quiet way, "I'd like to hear you call me by my first name . . . just once."

She placed her palms in a light caress along his cheeks, then studied his face, feature by feature. It was a strong, compelling face, holding the color of the sun and his heritage in its copper tone. Her fingertips rested just beside his black-lashed eyes, which were as splendid in this new seriousness as ever they were when laughing. His cheekbones were high, his nose straight. She rested her thumbs on his full lips and brushed the soft skin lightly.

In the gentlest of voices she said his name. "Sam . . . Sam . . . Sam . . . I want you inside me again, Sam. You feel so good there." She drew his face down to hers, her mouth opening to receive his kiss as he moved over her, fitting his hips to hers, his firmness to her pliancy. Her eyes closed as his flesh stroked within hers—long, ardent strokes that took her back to that plane of rapture they'd shared more than once the night before.

"Open your eyes, Lee."

She opened them, losing herself in his brown, probing gaze that hovered just above her as their bodies blended rhythmically together. They watched each other's faces mirror what was happening inside as they moved closer to glory, reveling in not only what they took but also in what they gave.

As Lee witnessed a parade of feelings cross Sam's face, she found new meaning in the act, and realized with utter certainty that it was not one into which he had entered lightly.

When it was over and her hands had brushed away the sheen of moisture from Sam's back, she gathered him close, wondering if he would understand that what she'd just experienced seemed a blending of spirits as well as of bodies. Holding him tightly, she whispered against his neck, "Oh, we are good together, aren't we, Sam?"

"Yes we are, Cherokee. I told you that last night." He braced his elbows on either side of her, and his thumbs smoothed her hairline, and once again they assessed each other, but looking deeper now.

"I'm glad it wasn't just me," she began. "I mean . . . I needed this very badly and I thought maybe that's why it was . . . exceptional."

He smiled and kissed the side of her nose. "No, it wasn't just you. It was exceptional for me too."

Her heart seemed to soar. "Was it really? You're not just saying that to be gallant?"

"Shall I stick around and convince you of that too?"

"Oh yes, Your Honor, please do."

And he did. They spent the weekend together, laughing and loving and learning about each other. And she came to know Sam Brown as a man of many facets.

That morning he insisted that she join him on an early run and produced from the trunk of his car a tote bag containing the same jogging clothes she'd seen once before. When she argued that it was Saturday, she had to clean the house, he said he'd help her when they got back. When she argued that she was out of shape, he said running would get her in shape—though he wasn't complaining. When she argued that it was hot, he said he'd cool her off.

They put on their sweatbands and headed out.

After a quarter of a mile Lee was lagging and panting. After half a mile her muscles burned. After that she tried to put her misery out of her mind, realizing what self-discipline it took to exercise like this every day. Her head hung. Her legs felt like deflated inner tubes. She followed Sam blindly, trailing doggedly at his heels and watching the slap of her feet . . .

He led her smack through the lawn sprinklers of Turner Golf Course!

She shrieked and threw her arms up over her head as the icy water brought her to a halt. "Brown, you're crazy!"

Still jogging, he turned to look at her over his shoulder. "I told you I'd cool you off," he called, then continued unceremoniously through the line of sprinklers. What could she do but laugh and follow?

When they returned home, he was the essence of solicitousness, laying her out on her stomach on the living room floor, then massaging her weary muscles with expert hands and soothing care. With her eyes closed and her cheek pressed against her crossed hands, she moaned, "Oh, Brown, how could you put me through that?"

"It'll keep you from getting fat and decadent," he replied cheerily, then completed her rubdown but refused to let her bask on the floor any longer. With a sharp slap on the rump, he ordered, "You have to keep moving or those muscles will tighten up."

With a groan she dragged herself up off the floor only to be hauled toward the shower. Without a flicker of embarrassment he joined her, and though it started out with Lee insisting she couldn't stand up for another minute, it ended with her soap-slicked body pressed flat against the cold ceramic tile and one knee hooked over Sam Brown's arm.

Afterward he made her breakfast, an ungodly concoction he called a Chinese omelette, declaring he had a passion for bean sprouts and water chestnuts. It was delicious after all, and the first meal a man had ever prepared for Lee. While they lounged at the table over cups of tea, Sam tipped his chair back on two legs, stretched a long arm toward the telephone on the counter behind him, called his mother, keeping his eyes on Lee all the time.

"Thought you might be worried," was the gist of his message.

When he'd hung up, he explained without compunction, "We don't interfere in each other's lives, but we share the same house. She'd do the same for me if she planned to be gone for an entire weekend."

And again, Lee looked at Sam in a new light.

There followed yet another surprise, for he was as good as his word and helped her with the house cleaning, showing an amazing lack of macho ego as he pushed the vacuum cleaner and emptied garbage cans. Joel had considered it "woman's work" and had never helped her with domestic tasks. Yet watching Sam Brown performing them now seemed to add to his masculinity rather than detract from it. She promised him a reward for his help and fulfilled that promise on the long sofa in the newly cleaned living room.

In the afternoon she remembered she'd made an appointment at the garage to have the oil changed in the Pinto. "Why not do it in the company shop and save yourself some money?" Sam suggested.

"Who, me?" she asked, surprised.

"Why not? The shop's got a hoist and any tools you need. Most of the guys who work for me take advantage of it. I don't mind."

"But . . ."

He leaned against the counter, crossed his arms, and cocked a dark eyebrow. "Don't tell me you're going to say, 'But I'm a woman.' Not after I just finished your vacuuming."

He had her there. She bit her tongue.

"I'll show you how, if you want me to. It's not hard," he offered.

And so Lee found herself doing the last thing in the world she'd ever have thought she'd do with Sam Brown—learning to buy the right size oil filter, the right weight oil; removing a drain plug, applying an oil-filter wrench, replacing the filter, then the plug, and finally the oil, and saving herself a considerable amount of money. And all at the suggestion of a man she'd once called rich and decadent.

But best of all, she'd earned Sam's respect, for as they headed back to her house, she knew he was pleased at the pluckiness she'd shown in her first attempt at auto maintenance.

They were scrubbing their hands at the bathroom sink when she looked up to find his approving eyes on her in the mirror. This time it was *he* who promised *her* a reward for her bravery, though he added with a charming grin that it would be the first time he'd ever made love to a mechanic.

While he went out to pick up a pizza, the "mechanic" prepared a homecoming.

Sam returned to a sight that stopped him dead in his tracks just inside the door. Lee posed at the far end of the hall haloed by the golden sunset coming through the patio door behind her. Her feet were bare. Her hair was loose. There were feathers in her ears and a white band around her forehead. Her palms rested on the walls above and beside her head while she slung her weight on one hip and the opposite thigh jutted forward. She wore nothing but a supple suede vest made up chiefly of swinging fringe. Several strands rode between her legs at the dark triangle of hair.

"Cherokee . . ." Sam breathed.

"Just so you don't get too used to me in a grease pit with a wrench in my hand."

"Come here, Cherokee," he said huskily.

They ate cold pizza.

A T three o'clock in the morning Lee awakened with a charley horse in her leg and sprang up in pain. Sam was immediately at the foot of the bed, taking her calf in his hands and working the heel to ease the cramping muscles until the spasms passed.

"Better now, sweetheart?"

She sighed and relaxed. "Mmm-humm." His hands were like magic, soothing away the hurt. He'd called her sweetheart. She lay back, relaxed, letting him massage and manipulate the cramp away, thinking of what a study in contrasts Sam Brown had turned out to be. As if to bear out the point, a few minutes later he eased himself beside her again and pulled her into the curve of his body until they rested like two spoons in a drawer. As if to himself he mused, "Well, well . . . what's this now? I think I've discovered an Indian mound."

Lee burst out laughing and swatted him. "Sam Brown, you're awful!"

"Mmm . . . maybe I'll explore it."

"This one's been explored several times today."

"What? No more treasures left in it?"

Already he was searching for anything he might have missed. She knew that when he found it delight would surely follow, so she teased in return. "Well, there might be an old arrowhead left lying around."

Within minutes she had completely forgotten the lingering discomfort in her leg.

THEY ran again the next morning, then Lee cooked Sam breakfast while he did the Sunday crossword puzzle. Afterward she was sitting on the patio brushing her hair when he surprised her yet again by kneeling behind her, taking the brush from her hand, and pulling it gently through the tangled locks. As he braided the dark strands, they talked about their families and their pasts.

But there was one topic Lee never discussed—her children. She kept the door closed on the extra bedroom, hoping Sam wouldn't ask questions. And he didn't . . . until late Sunday afternoon, when they were once again lying naked on the living room floor.

She had fallen asleep and awoke to find Sam stretched out on his side, watching her, his jaw braced on a palm.

"Hi," he greeted softly.

"Hi." She smiled. "What are you doing?"

"Waiting."

"Have you been waiting long?"

"Not long. It's been an enjoyable wait."

She wondered how long he'd been studying her and resisted the urge to hide her stomach behind an arm. Even before he moved, she sensed what he was wondering.

Still lounging on his side, he dropped his eyes and slowly lifted his dark hand from his hip. It moved toward her stomach, then a single fingertip traced the faded line there, following it downward from her navel.

"What's this?" he asked in the quietest of voices, lifting his eyes to hers.

She swallowed and felt a flash of dread, wanting to be honest with him yet searching for an adequate lie. Finding none, she could only answer, "It's a stretch mark."

"And what's it from?" His unsmiling eyes remained locked with hers.

The words stuck in her throat, though she realized he deserved an answer—an honest answer. He had seen the marks many times during the past two days but had refrained from asking questions until it became apparent she was not going to offer an explanation without being prompted. She swallowed dryly, her throat tight with apprehension.

"It's . . . it's from a baby I once had."

A long moment passed, rife with unspoken questions. Then, without another word, he bent to her, resting his lips against the telltale line. Lee's heart threatened to burst beyond the bonds of her body as his warm mouth lingered. Tears suddenly filled her eyes at the sight of him twisted from the hip, his shoulder blade outlined sharply while he breathed softly against her skin.

When he raised his head at last, it was to study her eyes deeply as he asked, "When?"

"A long time ago."

He touched his thumb to the wet track from a tear. "Tears again, Cherokee, just like that day in the orchard?"

His compassion never failed to throw her off guard, for it was so unlike what she'd first expected from him. She turned her head sharply aside and stared out the window, unable to meet the concern in his gaze any longer. But he stretched out beside her again, wrapped her in his strong arms, and forced her to face him.

"Did it die, Cherokee?"

The natural assumption. She knew she should dis-
abuse him of it here and now, but it was so hard . . .
so hard. She closed her eyes, trapping more tears that
wanted to escape, cutting off the sight of a tender,
concerned Sam Brown, whom she knew she was de-
ceiving by letting the misinterpretation go uncor-
rected.

"I can't talk about it. I . . . I just can't, Sam."

To Lee's surprise, he acquiesced. "Okay, we won't
talk about it now." He brushed the hair back from her
temple with his wide palm, then kissed the top of her
head. "Anyway, I think it's time I was going."

They were silent as they went upstairs and found
his clothes—the same he'd worn there Friday
night—and a robe for her. She walked him to the
door, but the gaiety they'd shared all weekend was
gone. They stood without speaking for a long moment, Lee staring at his feet, and Sam at the keys in
his palm. Finally he sighed and took her into his
arms.

"Listen, I have to fly to Chicago tomorrow. I'll be
gone for a few days."

She was taken by surprise at how abandoned his
announcement made her feel. They had spent two
days together—nothing more. How could she feel
this bereft after only two days?

Her arms circled his shoulders, suddenly strong
and clinging as she raised up on tiptoe, but after a

brief return of the pressure, he backed away and grinned down at her.

"Promise me you'll run every day without me?"

She dredged up a bright smile. "Promise."

He kissed her lightly. "I'll be back on Thursday or so." Again they fell silent. He drew in a deep breath and looked as if he were coming to a decision he didn't like. "It'll probably be good for us to be apart for a while, huh?"

"Sure," she agreed with that same false brightness, while her heart seemed to crack around the edges.

He gave her a last smile. "Get some sleep. You look exhausted."

Then he turned toward the door, and she found herself gripping its edge with both hands while calling after him, "Call me when you get back?"

"Of course."

BUT during the days that followed she wondered if he really would call. Why had that last conversation come up? *Why?* Each time she thought of it she felt like a fist was gripping her heart. He had guessed the truth, she was sure. He had guessed and wanted her to admit it, but when she'd backed away he'd decided it was time to take a second look at things. That's what he was doing on this trip to Chicago—evaluating her from a distance.

She lived with the fear that he would return having decided he didn't want to invest any more time in a woman who couldn't be totally honest with him, and she promised herself that if he called when he got back, she'd tell him the truth immediately.

In that brief time he had made himself an integral part of her life. He lingered in almost every corner of it—in the office, where she often glanced toward his open door, wondering how his business was going in Chicago, who he was with, if he missed her too; in her townhouse, where they had laughed and slept and made love and left memories in nearly every room; in her car, which reminded her of what fun it had been learning from him. Even running through the warm August evenings reminded her that he had already encouraged this change in her lifestyle, for she kept her promise and jogged after work each day, improving her wind control by breathing in long draughts as he'd taught her instead of in rhythm with her footsteps.

Sometimes she asked herself if this sudden obsession with Sam Brown was only sexual. Was she nothing more than a desperate divorcee who'd tumbled for the first man who gave her a second look? The idea frightened her, for ever since her divorce she'd feared doing that. Was she that kind of woman? Admittedly, it had been a long dry spell for her, which she'd certainly made up for with Sam Brown. Yet, what they had experienced that weekend had taken her feelings for him far beyond the sexual.

He had revealed himself to be a caring person, self-disciplined, amusing, devoted, compassionate, honest. What a surprise to discover such a myriad of admirable qualities hidden beneath the surface person she'd so mistrusted at first.

Recalling his attributes, she grew to miss him in a sometimes terrifying way and wished he'd call. But he didn't, though he checked in with Rachael every day. In a way Lee was hurt that he didn't ask to speak to her, but he'd said it would be good for them to be apart, and apparently he was giving the test a full chance.

Lee found him on her mind far, far too often and realized things had happened very fast between them. Too fast—like the first time with Joel when neither of them had stopped to think past the here and now. Hadn't she learned her lesson then? Yet here she was, plunged into loneliness over Sam after only a two-day relationship.

Relationship. She considered the word. Yes, she admitted, she and Sam Brown had related to one another in many ways. That was why their last conversation had come to bear such great significance and why his parting mood had left her utterly despondent. Once again she promised herself that the minute he called she'd tell him the truth.

Every time the phone rang in the office on Thursday, Lee's eyes went to the lighted button, wondering if it was him. Every time somebody's shadow crossed the doorway, she looked up with her heart in her throat. But he hadn't returned by five o'clock, and she drove home trying to decide whether or not she should run. What if he called while she was gone? In the end she kept her promise and went for the longest run she'd taken yet, pushing herself until her hip sockets ached and her thigh muscles quivered. Back home, she showered and put on faded blue jeans and a T-shirt with an advertisement for Water Products Company on its front. If he didn't call, if he didn't come, at least she wouldn't find herself at the end of the evening removing clothing that indicated she'd fussed and waited for him. But she polished her nails and braided her hair and put on a new brand of perfume she'd chosen for its light, uncloying scent. She opened the refrigerator perhaps a dozen times, but nothing appealed to her. She rehearsed exactly how she'd tell him, but each time she said the words her palms grew damp.

When the phone rang at 7:45, her heart seemed to skitter to her throat and her stomach went fluttery. It rang again. She lurched and grabbed it.

"Hello?"

Sam's baritone voice held an unexpected teasing note as he announced, "This is a collect obscene phone call from the Honorable Sam Brown to Cherokee Walker. Will she accept the charges?"

Joy sluiced through Lee, bringing a faint weakness to her knees. She beamed at the ceiling and answered, "Yes, she will."

"And is this Cherokee Walker?"

"It is."

"The one with the Indian braid on cleaning day and the mole way low on the left side of her rump?"

"Yes." A gurgle of laughter escaped her lips.

"And the one with the neat, sexy breasts just about the size of the palm of my hand?"

"The same." This was obviously no time for serious matters.

"The one who makes love on the living room floor and against the bathroom wall?"

"Sam, where are you?"

"I'm home, but I'll be at your house in exactly"— a pause followed as if he were checking his watch— "thirteen and a half minutes."

Her heart was hammering against her ribs, and she was smiling fit to kill. She was so relieved she forgot to say anything.

"Cherokee, are you still there?"

"Yes . . . yes, I'm still here."

Silence hummed for a moment before his voice came low and husky. "I missed you to beat hell, babe."

A great outthrusting pressure formed across her chest as she held the receiver in both hands and returned in a half whisper, "I missed you too. Hurry, Sam."

When had she last felt this giddy, this impatient? She was fifteen years old again, waiting for that special boy to walk into English class. She was sixteen, planning an appealing pose that a certain boy couldn't help but notice. She was seventeen and trying to appear casual while every nerve and muscle in her body was taut with anticipation. She conjured up the image of Sam Brown, and it was flawless and godlike, and she told herself it was only her breathless eagerness that made him perfect in her memory. Yet when reality stepped through her door, the memory paled in comparison.

He came in without knocking. She was standing at the kitchen end of the hall, where she waited for his knock after hearing the car door shut. At his unannounced entry, she drew in a quick breath, then stood unmoving, staring at Sam as he hesitated with his hand on the door—copper skin, chestnut hair, trousers of cinnamon brown, an open-throated ivory dress shirt, and a look in his dark eyes that said the past four days had been as long for him as they'd been for her.

"Cherokee . . ."

"Sam . . ."

She felt a moment of intense elation, took a hesitant

step, and then they were flying toward each other and
his arms were around her and hers were about his
neck as he lifted her from the floor and turned in a
joyous circle, holding her crushed high against his
chest with her nose pressed against his crisp collar,
where the scent of him was just as she remembered.
She closed her eyes, the better to absorb the almost
dizzying satisfaction at having him back again.
Sam . . . Sam. . . . He let her slip down, and even before her toes touched the floor, they were kissing,
with pounding hearts pressed together so tightly they
seemed to beat within a single body. Their tongues
conveyed not only impatience, not only eagerness,
but also that far more poignant message—you're as
good as I remembered . . . even better. She held the
back of his head in two greedy palms, felt it move as
his mouth worked compellingly upon hers and his
strong arms circled so far around her ribs that his fingertips touched the soft swells at the sides of her
breasts. Then his palms ran the length of her back,
caressing it through the T-shirt from neck to waist in
a touch that was curiously unsexual, but a confirma-
tion of her presence in his arms once again, a celebration at having her back where she belonged.

In much the same way she slipped her fingers inside the back of his collar, seeking warm skin, knead-
ing the hard knots of his neck as if to reaffirm his
presence.

When the first wild rush of greeting had finally passed, he lifted his head and his voice shook. "God, I missed you."

His words sent shudders of relief down her spine. His hands slipped under her shirt, and he folded his elbows along the center of her back till his wide palms came up through the neck of her T-shirt to cradle her head. She lay back against them, looking up at him, taking her fill of him.

"I missed you too . . . incredibly." Words seemed inadequate to describe how all-consuming her thoughts of him had been. She touched him in an effort to tell him in another way what her days had been like without him. She caressed his cheeks, his eyebrows, his lips . . . and as she did, his fingers massaged her head on either side of the thick braid. He closed his eyes and turned his parted lips against her fingertips as they brushed past.

"Chicago was almost a lost cause. I couldn't keep my mind on business," he confessed, still with his eyes closed, still with his lips turned against her fingers.

"The office wasn't the same without you."

He opened his eyes again. They held the look of a man who had truly come home.

"Wasn't it?"

She shook her head no. "I almost hated being there."

He smiled. "I'm glad. Misery loves company."

"Every time I knew Rachael had talked to you, I *was* miserable."

"Good, because I was too." His eyes wandered up to her hairline then, and his hands slipped from under her shirt to bracket her hips and settle them comfortably against his own.

"Did you run, like you promised?"

She laced her fingers around the back of his neck, leaning at the waist. "I ran like a dervish, trying to get you off my mind."

"Did it work?" The well-remembered grin was back.

"No." She squeezed his neck briefly. "It only made matters worse. But you'd be proud of me. I must have gone three miles today."

"Three miles! Hey, that's good." At his approval she was suddenly very, very glad she'd persevered with the running and felt a great rush of pride.

"Oh, and I went shopping, too, and got some decent running shoes."

He backed away and looked down at her feet. "Let's see—oh, very nice. No more charley horses?" He settled her back where she'd been and ran his hands idly over the curve of her spine.

"Nope. I'm getting tougher all the time." Again she thrilled at his grin of approval. Then he observed, "You shopped for something else while I was gone too, didn't you?"

"What?"

His head dipped briefly to her neck while his hands moved unhurriedly over her buttocks. "Some new perfume, I think."

"Do you like it?"

"Aha." His lips confirmed the answer with a soft nip at the skin beneath one ear.

"And it doesn't make you sneeze?"

"Un-uh."

She rocked lazily against him, smiling to herself while her fingers remained locked at the back of his neck.

"Good, because after the shoes I can't afford to try another kind."

He laughed, lifting his head, white teeth flashing, then asked, "Have you eaten yet?"

"No, and I'm ravenous now that you're back."

"So am I. Let's go get something, and you can fill me in on everything that went on around the office while I was gone."

"I'm not exactly dressed . . ." She backed away, tugging at the hem of the baggy T-shirt and looking down at it critically.

"You look sensational to me." Sam turned her toward the door, looped an arm over her shoulders, and gave her a nudge. "Now, let's get this damn eating over with so I can bring you back home and tell you again how much I missed you."

It wasn't until later that Lee realized the subtle change that had come over their relationship with Sam's homecoming. When it struck her, the significance was overwhelming. They had taken the time to catch up on each other's lives, talk business, eat supper together—all before they'd made love. And each moment had been equally satisfying.

Chapter
TEN

As August lengthened, Lee and Sam grew used to seeing each other every day at the office and every evening, in private, but in spite of Lee's silent promises, she never brought up the subject of her children. Somehow the proper moment didn't present itself that first night, and as the days slipped by it became easier and easier to put it off.

Yet she saw more and more of Sam. She learned his favorite foods, favorite colors, favorite movie stars. They attended an outdoor concert at the Starlight Theater, and he helped her pick out chairs for her living room. They went to a preseason game of the Kansas City Chiefs at plush Arrowhead Stadium and ran together almost daily.

On the surface everything was calm, and their relationship thrived. But as the last week of August neared, an undeniable tension grew between them. Sam had never asked why she needed the week off, but she knew he wondered.

There were countless times when she could have told him, such as when he'd scooped up P. Ewing, looked the cat in the eye, and said, "Cat, I like your name. Where'd you get it?"

It was the perfect lead-in, so why didn't she take the opportunity to explain that it had come from Jed, who'd inadvertently stumbled upon it by exclaiming the kitten was "pew-ing" the first time it used the sandbox?

It would have been so much simpler had she listened to her conscience and told him in the beginning. But the longer she held the secret inside, the bigger it grew, until it lay like a malignancy she knew must be removed before it eventually killed her. But by now she'd put off telling him for so long that she'd become paranoid about it.

There were times when she looked up to find Sam's eyes studying her pensively, and she knew he was biting his tongue to keep from asking the question which by now he had every right to ask. Yet, honorably, he didn't. And the tension built . . . and built.

Until the night he took her to his home to have dinner with his mother. The evening was an unqualified success, and Lee realized it represented another step in their deepening relationship. But she knew too that Sam had not chosen this last evening before her week off without due consideration. He'd done it as if to say—there, another obstacle overcome; now it's your turn.

All the way home in the car tension grew between them. Outside, a storm raged with great slashes of lightning zagging over the plains followed by awesome thunderclaps. Rain pelted down. The windshield wipers beat out a rhythm and the tires hissed through the rainy streets while inside the car Sam refrained from taking Lee's hand, which he usually did when he drove.

At the townhouse he killed the engine and the lights, then laced his fingers on the steering wheel and stared straight ahead, as if waiting for an explanation.

"Lee—" he began at last.

But before he could get any farther, she interrupted, "There's no sense in two of us getting soaked. You stay here."

His silence seemed to say, "On our last night together?" Yet he continued brooding while the tension mounted still higher between them. Finally, unable to think of a graceful exit line, Lee leaned over and kissed his cheek. He sat as stiff as a ramrod, but as she reached for the door handle, his hand lashed out in the dark and grabbed her so roughly that she gasped. Immediately he loosened his grip, and his voice became contrite.

"Lee, I'm going to miss you."

"I . . . I'm going to miss you too." She waited breathlessly, but still he didn't ask the question, and still she didn't offer an explanation. She wanted so badly to be honest with him, but she was so afraid of looking inadequate in his eyes. The silence lengthened, and the tension in the car seemed ready to explode. Then, just when she thought she couldn't bear it another instant, Sam released her hand, sighed tiredly, and sank down against the seat. She searched his face in the shadows, and for a blinding second the car interior was lit by lightning. His eyes were closed, and he'd rolled his face away from her while he pinched the bridge of his nose.

"Lee, I'm not sure . . . no, let me start again." His hand fell away from his nose, but his voice was strained and held an undeniable note of weariness. "I think I love you, Lee."

It was the last thing she'd expected him to say. Tears sprang to her eyes, and her heart pounded. She reached for his hand on the seat between them, took it in both of hers, and lifted it to her mouth. It was more than a kiss she placed on the back of it. It was a taking in of the texture, warmth, and security of it. And it was an apology.

She straightened the long, lax fingers and pressed her cheek and eyebrow against his knuckles.

"Oh, Sam," she breathed sadly against his hand, then carried it to the side of her neck and pressed it beneath her jaw where the pulse raced. "I think I love you too."

Everything inside Lee's body felt as temptestuous as the storm outside. She ran her fingertips down his inner wrist and felt his wild pulse, but he sat as before, wedged low in the seat.

"What should we do about it?" he asked, and she knew it was as close as he would come to forcing her to tell him why she was about to drop mysteriously out of his life for a week.

"Wait and see. We both said we 'think.' "

But even to Lee, her answer sounded inadequate, and she sensed his frustration mounting. "Wait?" he snapped, anger boiling to the surface again as he demanded in a hard tone, "How long?" His fingers closed tightly around hers.

"Sam, let me go in."

He seemed to consider a moment, as if calculating the effect of his question before asking, "Can I come in with you?"

Immediately she let go of his hand. "No, Sam, not tonight."

"Why?" He sat up straighter and seemed to strain toward her.

"I . . ." But she couldn't explain it. She only knew it had something to do with the boys coming tomorrow and a feeling of her own unworthiness. But before she could conjure up an answer, his voice cut coldly through the tense space between them.

"All right then, come here." And before she could guess his intentions, he reached for her in an insolent way he'd never before used with her and pulled her roughly across the seat until she fell against his chest. He began kissing her with a bruising lack of sensitivity.

"S . . . Sam, don't!" She struggled up, recoiling instinctively against him. But he grabbed her by both wrists, and he was frighteningly powerful in his anger as they poised, faced off in a half-prone position across the car seat. His fingers bit into the tender skin where her pulse raced. Tears trembled on her eyelids, and fear swelled up in her throat.

"Why do you pull away? I'm wishing the lady good-bye, that's all."

"Sam . . ." But before more words escaped her stiff lips, she was flung backward against his hard chest with her right hand wrenched between their bodies, rendering it useless. And all the while his voice grated near her ear. "I've just said I think I love you, and you told me the same thing. Considering that, I think you deserve a proper good-bye." She fought him with her single free hand, but he controlled it with amazingly little difficulty as he roughly opened the front fastening of her slacks and plunged his hand inside.

"Sam . . . why . . . why are you doing . . . this?" she sobbed.

But he was relentless. "Why?" His hand invaded the part of her body he had never touched with anything but utmost tenderness, but his voice made a mockery of the act. "This is what you keep me around for, isn't it? This is what you want me for, isn't it?"

He plundered her with consummate skill while an unspeakable sense of loss washed over Lee. She was sobbing quietly now, and somewhere in the back of her mind she knew she'd brought on this anger herself, for his confession of love had been an invitation for her to confide in him, yet she'd refused once again. Tears ran down her face as she finally gave up struggling and lay passively on his hard, aroused body, letting him do with her what he would.

But just as swiftly as it had come, the fight went out of him. His hand fell still while his chest still heaved with emotion. His heartbeat reverberated through the thin fabric of Lee's blouse, and he swallowed convulsively. At the sound, she too choked back the thick tears that clotted her throat. Slowly his fingertips withdrew to rest on the soft, warm skin of her stomach. Neither of them spoke.

In those moments, as she lay upon him, feeling him breathe torturously against the back of her neck, she saw the death of a love that might have been. She held back the sobs she wanted to release for the annihilation of something they'd built slowly and carefully, something that had shown such bright promise only a short time ago.

And—oh God, oh God—it hurt.

He had seized upon one of her greatest vulnerabilities and used it against her, knowing full well that his accusation would debase her. She wished she could go back ten minutes and live them again. But she could only fling the back of a wrist over her eyes while her throat muscles worked spasmodically. All the while she lay on top of him like a plucked flower, wilted by the very sun that had once given it life.

She opened her eyes and stared unseeingly at the rivulets of rain oozing down the windshield, turning an unearthly green in the intermittent flashes of lightning. For a minute she felt disoriented and removed from herself.

Then she summoned up the will to move and pulled herself up, slowly, slowly, sitting on his sprawled thighs and running shaky fingers through her tousled hair, unable yet to find the strength to remove herself from him completely.

"Cherokee—"

"Don't!" His rasping utterance was cut in half by

the stiffening of her shoulders and the harsh word. She had thrown up a hand in warning but still sat on him, still with her back to him. There followed a deadly silence, broken only by the ongoing thrum of rain on the roof and low growls of thunder.

Then, muscle by muscle, she dragged her weary body to the far side of the seat and untangled her legs from his. In the same deliberate fashion he righted himself behind the wheel, then hung his hands on it, staring straight ahead for several seconds before slowly lowering his forehead onto his knuckles.

She tucked in her blouse, zipped and buttoned her slacks, and reached to slip her shoes from her feet, all with the stilted motions of an automaton. But when she reached for her purse and then for the door handle, Sam lifted his head and placed a detaining hand on her arm.

"Cherokee, I'm sorry. Let's talk about this."

"Don't touch me," she said lifelessly. "And don't call me Cherokee."

His hand fell away, but his voice held a note of entreaty. "This happened because you won't confide in me. If you go in now and stubbornly refuse to—"

The car door cut off his appeal as she stepped out into the torrents of rain and slammed it shut. A river of water rushed along the curb, but she scarcely felt it as her nylon-clad foot splashed through it. Then she was fleeing blindly toward the door. Behind her the engine started up, and the car tore away at breakneck speed, the tail lights fishtailing down the street on the slick pavement. At the stop sign up the block he only slowed, then tore off again with a second screech of tires and swerving of tail lights that bled off into the distance.

THE night that followed was one of the worst in Lee's life. She was left utterly decimated by the rift between her and Sam while at the same time she realized she must buck up her spirits to face her sons. She damned Sam Brown for bringing this emotional turmoil into her life at a time that was already rife with it. Facing the boys brought again that sick-sweet lifting of the heart that was half joy, half pain, and as she knelt to greet them, it was with a foreknowledge that this visit was somehow doomed from the start.

Jed and Matthew had grown so much since she'd seen them. At six and eight, they now resisted her hello hugs. Telling herself not to feel slighted, she backed off, realizing she seemed strange to them and that it would take them a while to warm up. They loved her new townhouse, though, and claimed their new beds with exuberance and a few surprised "wows." They fell upon P. Ewing, seeming to have missed him more than their mother, and she looked on with heart-sick emptiness, remembering how she and Joel had decided to get the cat because they'd been fighting more and more and thought the pet would be good for the boys.

Daddy, they said, was fine, and they liked his new wife, Tisha, real good. Tisha made the best lasagna in the world. No, Lee answered her younger son when he asked, she wasn't too handy at lasagna. How about spaghetti? But it seemed Matthew had lost the fetish for spaghetti she remembered.

They squealed with glee at her suggestion that she take them to a pro football game the second day they were there. But they didn't know the Kansas City players' names and before long squirmed in their seats and became occasionally disruptive, teasing each other and punching playfully, their bouncing and boisterousness drawing unfavorable glances from people in nearby seats. They left the game after the third quarter. On the way home Lee learned that soccer was their favorite game now. Daddy was coaching their team, and Tisha came to every game.

On Monday Lee won their hearts by taking them on an all-day outing to Worlds of Fun amusement park. They rode the Zulu, Orient Express, and Scream-roller until Lee's feet hurt from standing around waiting. But after each ride she shared their renewed delight and robbed her pitifully poor pocketbook again and again for the junkfood they wanted. She forgot to bring suntan lotion, so by the end of the day the boys were both burned, thus irritable and uncomfortable in bed that night.

In her own bed, she thought about Sam and the day they'd ridden the Zambezi Zinger, but the day that had been so happy then only brought a bittersweet pang now and made her cry miserably. She missed him terribly, even while she hated him for the hurt he'd caused her. She considered calling him, but her emotional equilibrium was already strained to its limits by being with the boys again.

The boys. They hardly seemed like her sons anymore, and she felt increasingly inadequate. Nothing she did seemed right for their needs while everything Tisha did must be perfect. Tomorrow, she vowed, she'd make no mistakes.

That day she took them to the sixty-acre Swope Park Zoo with its six hundred animals. But they'd been to Florida's Busch Gardens last year and had ridden down the African Safari Ride, where elephants spray you while you go past. The Swope trip seemed a definite second best to her sons.

Each night when they were asleep in their twin beds, Lee stepped to the doorway of their room and studied the dark heads on the pale pillow cases, and tears clogged her throat. At those moments, the disastrous days paled and were forgotten. She was desperately happy to have them here. The two sleeping children were hers again, flesh of her flesh, beings of her making. She loved them in a terrifying way, yet knew with a keen, piercing certainty that their stepmother's love was far more influential than her own. Soon she would become a shadow figure to them. Perhaps she already was.

Matthew had a bad dream the next night and awakened in tears. She sat on the edge of the bed while the backs of his sunburned hands smeared tears across his cheeks and he cried, "Where's Mommy?"

"I'm here, darling," she answered soothingly.

But, disoriented and accustomed to the securities of his life in another home, he cried, "No-o-o, I want Mommy."

By Friday both Jed and Matthew were discussing their friends at home and making plans for what they were going to play when they got back.

On Saturday they produced money "Mommy" had given them to buy a gift for Daddy. Lee took them to the store of stores—Halls, in the Crown Center—where there were items like nowhere else in the world. They bought Daddy a bar of soap shaped like a microphone so that he could sing in the shower.

On Sunday Lee dressed them each in a brand new outfit she'd bought and waited anxiously for their father to come and pick them up. She wondered what her reaction to Joel would be and felt a quailing in her stomach as the doorbell rang. The boys catapulted to answer it. But with him they babbled mostly about all the exciting things they'd done during the week. It was to Tisha, waiting in the car, to whom they ran with arms extended.

Joel looked healthy and happy, watching the boys gallop across the lawn before he turned to her. She surveyed him with immense relief and realized he no longer posed a threat to her emotions. At some point she had stopped loving him, and she could face him now, comfortable with the fact.

"How are you, Lee?"

"Oh, I'm fine. Things are going well with my new job, and I've got the house now, and . . ." Her eyes wandered down the sidewalk to the boys, then back to Joel's face. "You and Tisha are doing a wonderful job with them, Joel."

"Thanks." He stood relaxed before her. "We're expecting another one in February."

"Well, congratulations!" She smiled. "I . . . well, please tell Tisha the same."

"I will." He made a move to leave and for the first time seemed slightly uncomfortable. "Well, I guess the guys will see you again at Christmas."

"Yes." The word sounded forlorn.

"Boys," Joel called, "come and kiss your mother good-bye."

They returned on the run, gave Lee the required

kiss, then forgot everything except getting back into the car as fast as they could.

When they were gone, Lee wandered about the house like a lost soul, hugging her arms. The kitchen smelled like cherry popsicles and she found one melting down the sink, dropped there hastily when she'd said their daddy had arrived. She picked up the stick and threw it away, then rinsed the red liquid down the drain. But the pink stain remained. She stared at it for a long, long time until it grew wavery. A tear dripped down and landed beside it on the almond-colored porcelain, and a moment later she leaned an elbow on the sink edge and sobbed wretchedly. The sound of her crying made her weep all the harder, echoing as it did into the empty room. *My babies.* She clutched her stomach and let misery overwhelm her, leaning her face against her forearm until it grew slick. Her sobbing became so choppy and prolonged that it robbed Lee of breath, and she felt her knees buckle. She moved to the kitchen table and fell into a chair, dropping her head forward on her arms, crying until she thought there could be no more moisture in her body. *Where's Mommy?* P. Ewing came and rubbed up against her leg and purred, bringing a renewed freshet of misery. She needed a tissue, but had none in the kitchen, so she stumbled upstairs and blew her nose and dried her eyes. Clutching a handful of soggy tissues against her nose and mouth, she leaned against the bedroom doorway and felt her grief renewed at the sight of the twin beds and the pennants on the wall above them. Her head fell tiredly against the doorframe, and she cried until her throat and chest ached. *I love you, Jed. I love you, Matthew.* Her misery seemed to have eternal life. The convulsive sobs continued until her head was bursting, and she dragged herself to the bathroom for two aspirins. But at the sight of her ravaged face in the mirror, more tears burned her swollen eyelids and she thought that if she didn't hear the sound of another human voice soon, she would most certainly die.

She stumbled down to the kitchen and dialed, seeking help from the only person who could solace her. When she heard his voice, she tried to calm her own, but she lost control and sucked in unexpected gulps of air in the middle of words.

"Ss . . . S . . . ham?"

A moment of silence, then his concerned voice, "Lee, is that you?"

"S . . . Sam . . ." She couldn't get anything else out.

"Lee, what's the matter?" He sounded panicked.

"Oh, S . . . Sam, I n . . . need you so b . . . bad." A huge sob broke from her as she clutched the receiver with both hands.

"Lee, are you hurt?"

"No . . . No, n . . . not hurt . . . j . . . just hurting. Please . . . c . . . come . . ."

"Where are you?"

"At h . . . home," she choked.

"I'm coming."

When the line clicked, her arm wilted toward the floor with the phone dangling from her lifeless fingers and she begged him, "Pl . . . please hurry."

She was sitting slumped over the kitchen table ten minutes later when Sam Brown ran up the walk and burst through the front door. He skidded to a halt in the middle of the hall, chest heaving. "Lee?" He caught sight of her as she flew out of her chair. They met in the middle of the hall. She flung herself against him, sobbing abjectly and clinging to his comforting body as she burrowed into him.

"S . . . Sam, oh, Sam . . . h . . . hold me."

He crushed her to him protectively. "Lee, what is it? Are you all right?"

Her body was heaving so much no answer was possible just then. He closed his eyes and pressed a cheek against her disheveled hair as hot tears melded his shirt and his collarbone. Her tormented body was wracked by shudders so he wound his arms around her tightly, waiting for her to calm down.

"Sam . . . Sam . . ." she sobbed wretchedly, over and over.

Never had a body felt so good. His hard chest and arms were a haven of familiarity. His scent and texture comforted immeasurably while he stood like a rock, his feet widespread, his long length shielding her. Forgotten were the hurts they'd caused each other. All forgotten was the pain of separation. Barriers fell as she sought his strength, and he gave it willingly.

"I'm here," he assured her, spanning the back of her head with a wide hand and pressing her securely to him. "Tell me."

"My b . . . boys, m . . . my babies," she choked, the simple words becoming an outpouring of her soul while he remained unflinching, the solid foundation of her life.

"They were here?"

She could only nod against his neck.

"And now they're gone?"

Again she nodded and felt him stroke her hair. She pulled back. "How l . . . long have you known?"

His hands spanned almost the entire circumference of her head while his thumbs stroked the tears that were her healing. "Almost since the beginning."

She looked up through a bleary haze while her heart swelled with love for him. "Oh, Sam, I was s . . . so afraid to t . . . tell you." She buried herself against him.

"Why?" His voice was thick, and she heard in it vestiges of the hurt she'd caused and promised herself she would make it up to him. "Couldn't you trust me?"

Fresh tears spouted again while she clung to him. "I was so af . . . afraid of what you'd th . . . think of me." Her shoulders shook even as relief overwhelmed her because he knew at last.

"Shh, don't cry. Come here." He pushed her back gently and slipped an arm around her shoulders, urging her toward the stairs. He sat down on the third step and tugged her down between his knees on the step below, then pulled her back against him. His broad forearm crossed her chest and hugged her tightly while he squeezed her upper arm and rested his chin against the top of her hair. "Now tell me everything."

"I wanted to tell you the l . . . last time we were together. I wanted to so badly, b . . . but I didn't know what you'd think about a . . . a mother who had her kids taken away from her in a divorce court."

His lips pressed the top of her head. "Darling, I saw their beds the first day I came here. I've been waiting since then for you to tell me about it."

"You've known all that time. Oh, Sam, why didn't you ask?"

"I did once, but you let me believe they had died, and I realized then that *you* had to tell me. And that last night we were together, I . . . oh God, Cherokee, I'm so sorry for what I did. But it damn near killed me that you couldn't trust me enough to tell me then. I've had a miserable week, thinking of how I've hurt you and wondering if my suspicions about your kids were right. At times I even found myself wondering if you were with your ex-husband, and I told myself if you were, it was no more than I deserved." His arm tightened perceptibly across her chest.

"No, not that. He's married again and they're expecting another baby."

"You saw him this week, too?"

"Yes, he came to pick up the boys just before I called you."

"They live with him, then?" His quiet questions encouraged her to talk about them, and she marveled at having a man who understood her needs so well. His warm palm caressed her bare arm, and his voice was very soft and compelling.

"What are their names?"

She brushed his forearm and felt his breath warm on the top of her head. "Jed and Matthew." Just pronouncing their names brought a sharp sense of renewed heartache. She sat quietly for a long moment, thinking of their empty beds upstairs. But she rested her head against Sam's chest and drew strength from him as she continued. "Oh, Sam, I don't know if I'll ever get over l . . . losing them. That day in the courtroom was like . . . like judgment day, and I've been in hell ever since. It was totally unexpected. My lawyer was just as dumbfounded as I was when the judge declared that he was giving custody of the boys to Joel. But Joel had a high-powered attorney, one he could afford, and I had a less experienced one that I couldn't afford. I just never dreamed I'd lose. My attorney kept telling me there was something called the 'tender years concept,' meaning basically that little kids need their mother. The boys were only three and five then. But the judge said the court found it would be in the best interest of the children to have a strong male role model." Lee pulled away from Sam's body, crossed her arms on her knees, and rested her head on them. "Male role model, for God's sake. I didn't even know what it meant."

Sam studied her back, reached to cup a hand over her shoulders, and pulled her securely between his legs again.

"Go on," he ordered quietly, slipping his arm across her collarbone.

She closed her eyes and swallowed, then continued in a strained voice. "His lawyer brought up the subject of economics, and mine argued, but it seems economics enter into the . . . the emotional well-being of children. I had no means of support, no career, no prospects. I'd been a wife raising babies, how could I have?" A shudder went through her. She swallowed and opened her eyes. Tears slipped down her cheeks, and a lump lodged in her throat.

"Oh, Sam . . . have you any idea wh . . . what it's like to have your children t . . . taken away? What a failure you f . . . feel like?"

A hot tear dropped on his arm. He squeezed her shoulders and chest in a bone-crushing gesture of comfort, resting his cheek against her hair. "You're not a failure," he whispered thickly. "Not to me . . . because I love you."

How many times this week had she longed for those words? Yet at the moment they tore at her soul, for it was because she loved him too that she wanted to be perfect in his eyes. But she wasn't—oh, she wasn't—so, she went on purging herself. "This week I realized I'm totally inadequate as a mother. The courts were probably right to take them away from me. She's done a better job than I ever could. I d . . . did everything wrong. I l . . . let them get s . . . sunburned and I—"

"Lee, stop it."

"I didn't know how to c . . . comfort Matthew when he had a b . . . bad dream and—"

"Lee!"

"And I . . . I . . ." The tears broke free again, and she struggled on in self-recrimination. "I c . . . can't m . . . make—" He grabbed her roughly and swung her around until her face was pressed against his chest where the last word came out a muffled sob— "lasagna."

"Oh God, Cherokee, don't do this to yourself."

"I d . . . did. everything wrong." She clung to the back of his shirt, wailing out her pitiful litany.

"Shh . . ." He patted her hair and held her head tightly with both hands.

"They ran to h . . . her and f . . . forgot all about m . . . me when she . . ."

His mouth stopped her words. He had jerked her roughly up to him and held her now in an awkward embrace, twisted as she was at the waist while they perched on their two different steps. He kissed her savagely, then lifted his head and held her jaw as he studied her face.

"They've been away from you for a long time, and they're used to her now. That doesn't mean you're a failure. Don't blame yourself. It breaks my heart to see you like this."

And from the depths of her misery she realized what she had in Sam Brown. Strength, understanding, compassion. Her hurt was his hurt for he absorbed it and his eyes became a reflection of the pain he saw in hers. She trembled on the brink of understanding the true depth of love. And, not wanting to put him through more agony, she finally made a shaky effort to control her tears. When they eventually lessened, he pushed her gently away from him, but only far enough to raise one hip and pull a handkerchief from his back pocket. When she'd dried her eyes and blown her nose, she felt better. Heaving a giant sigh, she sat down beside him on the same step. Bracing both elbows on her knees, Lee gingerly covered her burning eyelids with her fingertips and declared unsteadily, "My eyes hurt. I haven't cried this much since the divorce."

"Then you needed it."

She lowered her hands and looked at his understanding face.

"I'm sorry I unloaded on you. But thank you for . . . for being here. I needed you so much, Sam."

He studied her swollen eyes with their red rims, the fingers behind which she hid her cheeks. He reached and took one of her hands and interlaced his fingers with hers. "That's what love is all about, being there when you need each other, isn't it?"

She touched his cheek with her free hand. "Sam . . ." she said, quiet now, overwhelmed by love for him, certain that what he said was true.

Their eyes held, then he turned a kiss into her palm. "Have you decided yet whether you love me or not?"

"I think I decided on the day you came over here in your jogging shorts."

A brief smile lifted his lips, then they fell serious again. He said quietly, "I'd like to hear you say it once, Lee."

They were sitting side by side in a curiously

childish position, holding hands with only the sides of their knees touching as she said into his eyes, "I love you, Sam Brown."

"Then let's get married."

Her startled eyes opened wide. She stared at him for a full ten seconds, then stammered, "G . . . get married!"

He gave her a lopsided grin. "Well, don't look so surprised, Cherokee. Not after the last wild and wonderful month we've spent together."

"B . . . but . . ."

"But what? I love you. You love me. We even *like* each other! We're both in the same line of work, have terrific senses of humor, and we're even the same breed. What could make more sense?"

"But I'm not ready to get married again. I . . ." She looked away. "I tried it once and look what it's put me through."

"Cherokee, you're not going to go through this again, not if you marry me."

"Sam, please . . ."

"Please?" His voice took on an edge. "Please what?"

"Please don't ask. Let's just keep things as they are."

"As they are? You mean sex every night at your house and nothing more than a polite hello at the office? I said I love you, Lee. I've never said it to another woman. I want to live with you and hang our clothes in the same closet and have a family to—"

"A family!" She jumped off the step and stood at his feet facing him. "Haven't you heard a thing I've said? I had that once, and it was the worst tragedy of my life! I lost my sons—the only ones I ever plan to have—in a divorce court. I'm not equipped to be a mother. I told you that!"

"That's all in your head, Lee. You'll be as good a mother as—"

"It's not in my head!" She swung away toward the living room. "I . . . I'm insecure and hurt, and I've failed once at being both a wife and a mother. I don't think I'd be very good at either one again."

He stood behind her in the middle of the living room.

"That's your answer, then? You won't marry me because you're afraid?"

She swallowed and felt the damnable tears spring to her eyes again. "Yes, Sam, that's my answer."

"Lee." He placed a hand on her shoulder, but she shrugged it away. "Lee, I won't accept it, not if you really love me. The only way to get over being afraid of something is to try it again. You're . . . we're not going to fail. We've got too damn much going for us. I just know it."

"It's out of the question, Sam. I just don't understand how you . . ." She turned to face him. "Sam, you can't know how a thing like losing your children can undermine your self-confidence. I swore when it happened that I'd never go through such a thing again. I'd prove to the world that the judge was wrong. I wasn't just a . . . a stupid *squaw* with . . . with no career and no visible earning power. I had things to prove, and I'm not done proving them yet."

"Squaw?" he retorted angrily. "Is that what this is all about?"

"It's part of it. Nobody will ever convince me that judge wasn't influenced against me because I was Indian and Joel wasn't. It has as much to do with the decision as the fact that I couldn't support the kids. Well, I couldn't do anything about my heritage, but I certainly could about my financial status. I set out to earn as much money as any man, in a job only men have traditionally done, but I have a long way to go before I reach my goals."

Sam's face was grim. "Lee, you've got a red chip on your shoulder about the size of the original Indian nations! You carry it there, daring anybody to knock it off—that's why most people try. When are you going to learn you're melted into the pot here, and stop flaunting your heritage?"

Fresh anger flared through Lee. "You don't understand a thing I've said here today! Not a thing!"

"I understand it all, Lee. I'm just not willing to buy some of it. I love you and I accept you exactly as

231

you are, without any question that we could make a successful marriage—babies and all. You're the one who doesn't understand that if you really love somebody past histories should be forgotten and you should put your entire trust in the strength of that love."

She reached out to touch him, her face tight with pain. "I *do* love you, Sam, I do. But do I have to prove it by marrying you?" He removed her hand from his chest and held it in his own.

"That's the usual way, Lee." He looked up, and his dark eyes held a glint of hurt before he added softly, "The honorable way."

What could she say? After the way they'd parted last time, the hurts they both carried since then, how could she argue with him? She saw a grave weariness settle over his features as he stood holding her palm with the tips of his fingers, brushing his thumb across her knuckles.

She stared at him, already stricken with loss. "Sam, don't go."

Again she saw his weariness and the burden of sadness that her refusal had so suddenly brought upon him. He looked into her eyes, and his own were heavy with regret.

"I have to, Cherokee. This time I have to."

"Sam, I . . . I need you."

He stepped close again, drew up her face, and

placed a good-bye kiss on her lips, which were swollen yet from crying.

"Yes, I believe you do," came his tender reply.

He studied her black pupils, touched a thumb to the purple skin of one lower eyelid, then turned, and a moment later the door closed behind him.

Chapter
ELEVEN

F she were asked to define exactly who brought about the changes between them, Lee could not truthfully have named either Sam or herself. She only knew they'd reached an impasse that hurt deeply during the weeks that followed. Facing him each day at the office was sheer hell. He no longer passed her desk in the late afternoon to ask what time she'd be leaving for home. She no longer asked if he was coming over. Lee knew either of them could have broken down the invisible barrier that had sprung up between them. It would have taken no more than a single word, yet neither spoke it.

On the surface everything was the same. They consulted each other on bid work, bumped into each other in the copy room, pored over plans together. But through it all Sam maintained an incredibly un-fluctuating air of normalcy, while Lee gave him nei-ther pointed indifference nor veiled languishments. Instead they treated each other with neutral geniality, which made her wince inwardly. He opened doors for her if they were heading out together, and they chat-ted about jobs with a heartiness that distressed Lee's lovelorn soul.

One day in mid-September Sam passed her as she sat near the fountain eating lunch. He waved a roll of plans in greeting, never breaking stride as he called, "Hi, Lee. Enjoying the beautiful weather?" An acute sense of loss pierced her as she watched him stride purposefully into the building.

In late September six members of the office staff treated Rachael to a birthday lunch at Leona's Restau-rant in the Fairway Shops. They all piled into Sam's car for the short ride. Lee ended up in the back seat. Being there brought back memories of the days of in-timacy with distressing clarity as she studied the back of Sam's head.

At Leona's, Lee found herself seated at a right angle to him. As they pulled their chairs in, their knees collided under the table. "Oh, excuse me!" Sam apologized. "It's these damn long legs of mine." His alacrity was as impersonal as if he had bumped Frank's knee, and again Lee felt raw inside. Yet she heard herself laugh and copy his nonchalance.

But for Lee being with him became a refined form of torture. At times she studied him across a room, wondering if he had intentionally plotted this insipid neutrality to punish her. Was he aware of it? Did he maintain this jovial air knowing that every day now put her over the rack? Or had he simply chalked up their affair to experience and moved on to greener pastures? If he loved her, as he claimed he did, how could he be so . . . so damn mundane! When he caught her looking at him, he smiled and turned back to whatever he was doing without the slightest sign of constraint and certainly without flashing any intimate messages with his eyes. But then, did she herself flash any?

September crept to a close, and the first hint of fall tinged the air. Sam called Lee into his office one day, but again he was his ineffable genial self, announcing that she'd been there two months and he was giving her a raise because he was very pleased with her work. Though it was a small boost in pay, he said he meant it as a vote of confidence and ushered her to the open door, where they stood for a minute in full view of the draftsmen. He smelled so familiar that saliva pooled beneath Lee's tongue. The sight of his shirt-sleeves rolled up to the elbow, exposing summer-bronzed forearms, and the familiar way he slipped a hand into his trouser pocket as they talked, raised goosebumps of awareness across the low reaches of Lee's stomach.

Sam leaned against the door jamb and crossed his arms over his chest, discussing some aspect of the Little Blue River job, which was in full swing by this time. The apples in the orchard would be ripe now, the mosquitoes gone, the red-winged blackbirds and goldfinches flown south. *Oh, Sam, Sam, I haven't stopped loving you.* He continued to discuss business as if nothing had ever happened between them. *Sam . . . Your Honor . . . I want to reach for you, burrow against you, and be part of your life again.* It was time to make some major decisions about equipment, he was saying, while from Lee's body came both a physical and emotional outpouring of need for him. *How can you act as if it never happened when every nerve in my body feels touched by you?* ". . . so Rachael will make the plane reservations. Plan to be gone overnight," Sam was saying.

"I . . . what?" Lee stammered.

"Plan to be gone overnight," he repeated. "I just don't see how we can fly to Denver, attend the equipment auction, and get back here in one day, especially if we end up buying something. There'll be financial arrangements to make, and we'll have to find a yard to rent."

His words hit her like a blow in the stomach. He'd been standing there making plans for the two of them to attend the heavy-equipment auction in Denver with no more compunction than he'd announce the same to Frank or Ron or any of the other guys. Lord o' mercy, did he expect her to go off on an overnight jaunt with him and keep it totally platonic? What did he think she was made of ... PVC, like the pipes they laid in the ground? His lack of sensitivity infuriated her ... and the prospect of being alone with him left her weak and trembling.

THEY flew out of Kansas City on a golden mid-October day, and as the plane looped westward, leaving the cloverleaf design of K.C. International Airport behind them, Lee had a feeling of *déjà vu,* because they were going back to the same place where they'd met.

Before they crossed over mid-Kansas, Sam had slumped back and fallen asleep beside her. He woke up long enough to decline breakfast, leaving Lee to eat alone, ever aware of his slow, slumberous breathing at her shoulder, remembering mornings when she'd awakened to that sound on the other side of her bed. He was still sleeping peacefully when the seatbelt sign flashed on in preparation for landing. She studied his shuttered eyes, the long, dark lashes fanning his cheeks, his lips and limbs in repose, and a renewed sense of longing sprang up inside her. Hesitantly she touched his arm, which lay lax over the armrest between them.

"Sam?"

His eyes opened abruptly and looked directly into hers. There was a moment of disorientation, a sweet, compelling return to the days when they'd awakened together, a sensual smile of hello beginning to tip up his unwary mouth before he seemed to realize where he was and curbed the warm response.

"We'll be landing in a minute," Lee said, casting her eyes away when he clasped his hands, stiffened his elbows, and stretched, uncoiling and shivering in the old, familiar way.

"God, I slept like the dead," he said, reaching for his seat belt.

You always did, she wanted to say. Their elbows bumped when they were latching their buckles, and Lee wondered how she would survive this torture for two days.

Inside Stapleton International Airport they stood side by side, watching the luggage bump toward them, both reaching for the first familiar suitcase when it arrived. Lee backed off, letting Sam retrieve it and check its I.D. tag. "This one's yours," he stated, setting it at her ankle with no further comment or clue to what he was thinking. His suitcase arrived, and they set off to rent a car.

Sam stowed their identical suitcases in the trunk,

unlocked the passenger door, and waited while Lee
got in. How many times had he done this for her
when they were lovers? Yet now there was only the
impersonal politeness he'd show to any woman as a
matter of course. When he was behind the wheel Lee
was assaulted by the familiarity of his movements,
his scent, his hands on the steering wheel.

The auction was to be held at the Adams County
Fairgrounds in Henderson. By the time they arrived,
Lee was only too happy to escape the confines of the
car with its taunting reminders and inescapable memories. But the day proved as distressing as the ride,
for it was a remarkably mellow one, the kind in
which lovers revel. The Colorado sky was a cloudless
cerulean blue, none of Denver's usual brown haze
blocking out its deep color. The state's famed aspens
were at their peak of brightness too, shimmering
like golden coins beneath a butterscotch sun. Accom-
panying Sam, inspecting machinery, discussing the
needs of the company for the upcoming spring job
here where their relationship had begun, Lee had difficulty concentrating on business. Time and again she
drifted into thoughts of the man at her elbow—the
texture of his skin beneath the golden mountain sun;
the shadows of his shoulder blades under the knit
shirt that delineated the well-remembered shape of
his chest and arms; the sheen of his dark hair, which
she had first touched in a brush in a motel room not

far from where they now stood; the outline of his thigh muscles within his trousers, those muscles she'd first seen on her doorstep on a summer's morning that changed her life forever; his voice, which had spoken countless intimacies into her ear and soothed her shattered soul with reassurances when she'd most needed them.

Being alone with him this way yet not alone at all only tightened the string of emotional tension to a higher pitch, until Lee felt as if one more inadvertent nudge of his arm against hers would snap that tensile thread.

He bid on several pieces of machinery, bought two, and made arrangements for payment and pickup with the auctioneering company's financier.

By the time they made their way back toward the rented car, it was late afternoon and the Denver freeways were packed. Lee had no idea where they were staying, but feared Rachael might have made reservations at the Cherry Creek again. To her relief, Sam drove to a different hotel—an airport high-rise. They checked in side by side, but took two separate rooms. Sam extended his company credit card without the slightest hint of uneasiness. He handed Lee one of the keys, and they rode up to the ninth floor together. The hall was carpeted and silent as they moved toward adjacent doors.

Lee thought Sam might suggest meeting for dinner,

but instead he unlocked his door, glanced inside, and remarked casually, "Mmm . . . looks like a nice room." Then he picked up his suitcase, turned and answered the question that had been burning within her all day: "See you in the morning, Lee."

It would have been graceless and ill-advised to declare that she was lonely and missed his company and wanted terribly to spend the night with him. Instead she stepped into her own lonely cell and leaned weakly against the closed door to stare at the avocado green carpeting and matching bedspread without seeing either. What she saw was the face and hands and body of the man she loved, the man separated from her by a plaster wall and the equally as palpable barrier of their self-imposed strictures. To know he was there, so close, yet untouchable, was torture. While she stared at the lonely room, tears threatened. A tight constriction squeezed her chest. She crossed to the window and took in the view of the Denver skyline—the Great West Towers, Denver Square, and Anaconda Towers off in the distance. The sun was setting behind the Rockies, which appeared in the foreground like a triple-tiered Mexican skirt, fading from dark purple to light lavender in three distinct layers, from the earth skyward.

She turned away from the stunning view and fell across the bed, battling tears. *You know I love you, Sam. Why are you doing this to me?* When she cried, she felt better and got up to wash her face, refresh her makeup, and go down to dinner, since it was obvious Sam had no intention of asking her to join him for the meal.

As she ate in solitude, anger began to replace her hurt. Her ego smarted. *Damn you, Sam Brown, damn you! Damn you! Damn you!*

Back in her room, she flung her key down on the dresser and glared at the wall. A minute later she pressed her ear to it. She thought she could make out the sound of his T.V. but wasn't certain. She turned on her own, but it had no appeal whatsoever. She flounced onto her bed, plumping the pillows behind her back, but the short-lived anger had dissipated now, leaving her with despair and a crushing yearning that blotted out common sense.

At five minutes after nine o'clock she picked up the telephone and dialed Room 914.

"Yes?" he answered.

She closed her eyes and rested her hand against the headboard. Her heart beat like a tom-tom, and her tongue felt dry and swollen.

"Th . . . this is an obscene phone call from Room 912. W . . . will you pl . . . please come and . . . and . . ." But her voice faltered as she clutched the phone and swallowed.

"And what?"

Oh God, he wasn't going to help her at all. He was

going to keep up this sham. She swallowed her pride, closed her eyes, and admitted, "I was going to say and make love to me, but I need you for so many more reasons than that. I miss you so much that nothing is good in my life anymore."

She thought she heard him sigh tiredly and pictured him, perhaps leaning his back against the wall only inches behind her. The earth seemed to turn one complete revolution before he finally asked, "Are you sure now, Lee?"

Tears seeped from the corners of her eyes. "Oh, Sam, what have you been trying to do to me these past weeks?"

"Give you a chance to heal."

Through her misery she felt a first glimmer of hope. She let her eyes drift closed, realizing it was what she too had been doing.

"Sam, please . . . please come over here."

"Okay," he agreed softly, and hung up.

An instant later a soft tap sounded on her door.

When she'd opened it, she stepped far back, interlacing her fingers and pressing them against her stomach. They stared at each other for an interminable moment as he leaned a shoulder against the doorframe. He was dressed in black socks, gray trousers, and a pale blue dress shirt held together by a single button at the waist. The shirttails hung out of his pants and it looked disheveled, as did his hair.

"Were you asleep already?" Lee asked guiltily.

He shook his head tiredly, no. "I don't think I've slept for the last six weeks—except on that plane today." How had she failed to notice the pinched lines at the corners of his eyes and the tired droop of his mouth?

"Because of me?" she asked hopefully.

He pulled himself away from the doorframe and, with his head drooping forward, turned and slowly closed the door. His shoulders rose in a great sigh, and at last he faced her again. "What do you think?" he asked quietly.

She stared back at him, blinded by pain and tears that threatened to spill from her lashes. "I haven't known what to think since you walked out of my house that night. I . . . you . . . it's been . . ." Her palms flew to cover her face and sharp sobs jerked her shoulders. "I . . . I . . . love you so," she choked out against her hands.

He moved to stand before her, and his warm hands encircled her wrists, forcing them away from her face. He placed a gentle kiss on the heel of each, where salty tears had left them wet.

"I love you too," he said, his voice softened by pain.

With a small, throaty cry she flung herself against him, arms looping up to circle his neck and cling. His arms, too, clasped her tenaciously while he pressed his face against her warm neck. He rocked her back and forth, back and forth, standing with feet spread while holding her body firmly molded to his, neither of them speaking, drawing comfort from their nearness.

Her breasts, belly, and thighs flattened to his rigid body, Lee's mind seemed filled with his name—Sam, Sam, Sam—and the sweet realization that he was what she needed to complete not only her body but also her life, her *self*.

At last he raised his head and she hers. Their eyes delved, dark into darker, speaking of the ache each had borne during their separation, speaking of anguish about to end in triumph.

Their mouths met wordlessly and drank and sought to make up for the emptiness of six weeks alone. Silky, wet tongues twisted together, speaking of a want grown one hundredfold since last they'd touched. The kiss lasted for endless, reckless minutes—glorious! greedy!—until their hearts clamored and their blood pounded. Sam bit Lee lightly, and her tongue slid back to feel the texture of his teeth scraping atop and below it. Her fingers found the warm hollow behind his ear, and she made a throaty sound that sought to tell him everything she felt for him.

His palms slid to her hips, moving them securely against his own complementary curves. He pressed his face into the scented side of her neck and as she tipped her head aslant, he whispered roughly, "What are you doing with all these clothes on?"

Her heart seemed to trip over itself as she raised her lips to his ear and answered in a tremulous voice, "Waiting for you to ask me again to marry you."

His head lifted in surprise, and a smile tugged at the corners of his mouth. "Bring it up later, when we have nothing better to talk about."

Then he sobered again, running his eyes over her hair, face, and breasts in a sweeping glance that brought them back once more to the black, searching Cherokee eyes that were alight with love and longing.

He lifted her chin, and his face lowered, while with infinite tenderness he circled her lips with the tip of his tongue. Then they were kissing again, open-mouthed and seeking, while she felt the flutter of his fingers at the valley between her breasts.

He lifted his head, and their eyes met again, then dropped together to his bronze fingers that slipped buttons through holes, then tugged the blouse from the waistband of her slacks. Wordlessly he slid it from her shoulders. Wordlessly, too, he reached behind her and when he backed away again the white brassiere was draped over his dark hands. He tossed it behind her and looked down at her stomach. A moment later he had freed the button at her waist and lowered the zipper beneath it, revealing a wedge of skin above low-slung briefs. He dropped to one knee, pressing his face within the open garment, kissing her stomach where weeks ago he'd traced the line she was so afraid to explain. He traced it again, this time with the feather-light tip of his tongue.

"There's nothing I don't love about you . . . nothing," he vowed as his strong arms cinched her hips and his eyes slid closed. He turned the side of his face against her flesh while his voice grew gruff with emotion. "You never have to be afraid to tell me anything. Always remember that."

Tears trembled close to the surface as she twined her fingers in the hair at the back of his head and pressed him nearer. She closed her eyes against the sweet swelling sensations his words brought to her chest, welcoming the faintly abrasive scratch of his whiskers. The top of his hair brushed the undersides of her breasts, and she leaned low over his head, cradling it in both arms.

"Oh, Sam, I was so afraid to have you see those marks the first time. Afraid of your disapproval, and . . . and wanting to be perfect when I couldn't be. But that's what love does to you, makes you want to be flawless for the one you love."

He pulled back to look up at her. "Cherokee . . ." His dark eyes were eloquent with approval even before he spoke the words. "I wouldn't change a single thing about you, don't you know that?" He reached one dark hand up to cup a breast, lifting it slightly as he brushed its crest with his thumb, yet looking beyond it to her eyes.

And suddenly she did know it, just as she knew she loved this warm, complex man. She threaded the fingers of both hands back through the hair of his temples, then held the sides of his head while savoring the moment and him.

"I know," she finally breathed softly. Then she leaned to kiss his lips, lightly at first, but with growing ardor, until she felt his hands moving over her skin to the loosened waistband that was soon being eased over the backs of her thighs. When it threatened to trip her, he stood, his hands sliding up her ribs to her armpits until she felt herself being lifted into space. He held her effortlessly, his mouth teasing her jaw while she pressed her hands to his hard shoulders and kicked herself free of impediments. But when the clothes dropped to the floor, he still held her aloft.

"Sam, Sam, let me go," she said, feeling helpless and impatient, wriggled provocatively against him.

"Never." He smiled back, then she was sliding down his body, freeing the single button that held his shirt together at the waist. While he shrugged it off hastily, she loosened his belt buckle.

Suddenly she realized he was standing motionless, and her fingers fell still. She looked up to find him watching her with the faint hint of a smile on his lips.

How incredible that after all they'd been through she could feel this abrupt shyness, as if it were her first time. His hands hung loosely at his sides, and the expression on his face was a mixture of enjoyment and anticipation.

"Be my guest," he said softly.

Her lips fell open. A thrill spiraled through her while the breath seemed caught in her throat. Then she accepted his invitation, pulling the last garments from between them.

When they were naked, it took no more than a step and he was against her, forcing her back until her calves struck the bed and she toppled backward, pulling him with her. Their bodies were all grace and harmony while their mouths spoke wordless intimate messages and their hands roamed over each other, familiarizing themselves once again. "Oh, Sam, how I missed you." His shoulders were sleek and firm, his hair the texture of mink, the tendons of his neck resilient as she ran her hands over them. He leaned above her, kissing her temple, her eyelids, catching her lip between his teeth while her eyes drifted closed and she took pleasure in his adulation.

He moved down, turning them onto their sides while trailing kisses from the underside of her chin along her throat and down the hollow between her breasts, detouring to bestow a lingering kiss on each before moving on. His elbow hooked the curve of her waist, and his forearm pressed silkily against her back while he dipped a pleasurably wet tribute into her navel. He pressed her back, easing lower to trace once more those pale lines she no longer thought of hiding, learning their texture with the tip of his tongue.

"Cherokee . . ." His voice was rough, his lips soft while he nuzzled lower . . . and lower. "Cherokee . . ."

Then all was sensation—rough to smooth, ebb to flow, texture to sleekness, man to woman. She made some inarticulate sound deep in her throat, raising her body while drifting in an ethereal realm of sensuality.

He took her just short of fulfillment, then came to her, lifting himself over her once again to join the force of his love with hers in movements that were as much a part of love's expression as its innermost urge to give and to share.

Lee's head was thrown back, her eyes closed as she reached above her for something to hold on to, finding nothing but a pillow into which her fingers curled while he watched the pleasure in her trembling eyelids.

His name ripped from her throat as they shared again that shattering force of feeling they'd known before, followed by the dissolving sigh of satisfaction. A kiss on her forehead, the weight shifting away, taking her with it to her side, a heavy hand threaded through her hair, then a blissful lassitude as they lay in each other's arms.

"Cherokee?" he murmured after a long, long time.

"Hmm?"

His chest was warm and damp where her forehead rested against it.

"Can we talk now?"

"The answer is yes," she said, smiling at the ebullient feeling it gave her to say the word at last.

"The . . . what?" He jerked back in surprise.

"The answer is yes." She looked up innocently into his eyes. "Yes, I'll marry you. Yes, yes, yes!" She kissed his chest with a quick, light smack.

And naturally he had to tease, "I didn't ask you yet."

"You were gonna."

"Oh, was I now?"

She snuggled up against him, wrapping her arms around him and nestling comfortably with her head tucked under his chin.

He lifted a knee, rested it on her hip, and pressed the sole of his foot in the warm hollow at the back of her leg. "You know what I kept thinking the last six weeks?" His tone was reflective. "Of what a damn fool I was the night I asked you to marry me. My timing stank. I know that now. You were in an emotional mess that night, and I had no business bringing up the subject just then. I thought . . ." He sifted his fingers through her hair as if it were sand. "I thought I'd give you some time to gain your equilibrium after seeing your kids and your ex-husband again."

"You had me so scared, Sam." She squeezed her eyes shut, then hugged him close with fierce possessiveness. "I've never suffered as badly as I have during the last six weeks. You were so . . . so . . . unaffected by it all."

"Unaffected!" he exclaimed, pushing her back to see her face. "Woman, I was dying a little bit each day, waiting for you to come to me and say you'd changed your mind."

"You were?" She widened her eyes in surprise. "You didn't act like you were dying. You acted as if I was just one of the boys."

"Just one of the boys?" The grin was back as he ran his eyes then his hand over one naked breast. "Oh, Cherokee, hardly. It's not one of the boys I want to share my house with . . . and my life with . . . to say nothing of my bed."

She smiled and felt a ripple of feminine vanity at his approval.

Then she fell serious, gazing up at him with concern. "Sam, have you really no fears at all?"

He pressed a kiss to her forehead. "None. Not since that first incredible weekend with you when we found out how much we can share."

"But . . ." She searched his eyes deeply, hoping he wouldn't misconstrue what she was about to say. "I do have fears, Sam. Please understand."

"I know, Cherokee. I know now."

"At least give me some time before we start a family, okay?"

His head snapped back and he braced up on one palm, a dark hand grasping her shoulder and rolling her onto her back. "You mean it, Cherokee? You've been thinking about . . . about kids?"

"Yes, Your Honor, I have to confess I have." She affected a scolding pout. "Not right away, mind you. After I have a little time to get used to the idea."

His smile was radiant, then to her amazement he gave a regular Indian war whoop and fell on his back beside her, rubbing his chest with an air of great satisfaction and smiling up at the ceiling.

She lay beside him, grinning at how happy she'd made him, wondering what one of their half-Indian babies would look like. It would have hair darker than his, beautiful eyes, with his long lashes instead of her short, stubby ones, and the prettiest lips this side of the Great Divide . . .

Her reverie was interrupted by the growing awareness that Sam was no longer looking at the ceiling but at her naked breasts. The message in his eyes was clear even before a dark finger came teasing.

"Hey, Cherokee, what do you say we jump in the shower together and start all over and celebrate? I've got some time to make up for."

She burst out laughing and shoved his finger aside. "What have you been doing over there in your room all by yourself? Reading your porn magazines again?"

"How did you guess?"

She pretended to consider a minute. "On second thought, I'm not sure if I should hitch up for life with a man who reads porn magazines when he's got a perfectly capable wife." She sat up saucily and was heading for the edge of the bed when her progress was checked abruptly. A second later she squealed, "Brown! Let me go, Brown! I gotta go to the bathroom!"

"Not alone, Cherokee! You're going with me, straight to the shower!" In a flash she was slung ignominiously over his shoulder, her black hair dangling down past his posterior while one dark forearm clamped behind her knees and his other hand rested on her upturned derrière.

"Brown, put me down!"

"Like hell." He chuckled and stalked off toward the bathroom.

"Pervert!" she squawked.

"You damn betcha," he agreed, then turned to bite her enticing backside playfully as it bounced along on his shoulder.

She could hardly breathe by the time they reached the bathroom and he let her slip to her feet. She landed in the cold, hard bathtub, and a minute later the colder spray hit her full in the face. Before it warmed, they were kissing and slipping against each other and groping for the tiny bar of soap.

While Sam unwrapped it, she pushed her sodden hair out of her eyes.

"Hey, Brown, I've got just one more question, and I think I deserve an answer."

Disgruntled by the interruption, he curled his brows. "Okay, what—but hurry up and get it over with so we can get on with the important stuff."

"Did you read the amount of my bid that day we first met?"

A slow, sly grin climbed his cheek. He shut his eyes, leaned his head back till the shower spray hit him full in the face, then brought it forward, shook his head like a dog, and opened his spiky-lashed eyes again. "I'll tell you what." He pulled her up close, settled his hips against hers, and taunted with a grin, "You do *ev-v-v*erything I say and I'll think about answering that."

"Brown—" she started to scold playfully, but the word was cut in half by his wet lips, and a moment later the answer ceased to matter.

From the New York Times
bestselling author
LaVyrle Spencer

The red-hot novels of

SUZANNE CHAZIN

The Fourth Angel

0-515-13249-7

Flashover

0-515-13508-9

"WILL DO FOR FIREFIGHTING WHAT PATRICIA
CORNWELL DID FOR FORENSIC SCIENCE."
—LEE CHILD

"FASCINATING...EXPLORES NEW TERRITORY."
—CHICAGO TRIBUNE

"FRIGHTENINGLY VIVID."
—PUBLISHERS WEEKLY

Ignite your imagination.
Pick up a copy wherever books are sold or at
www.penguin.com

ELIZABETH BERG